# A SON FOR THE ALIEN WARRIOR

TREASURED BY THE ALIEN 2

HONEY PHILLIPS

BEX MCLYNN

Copyright © 2019 by Honey Phillips and Bex McLynn

All rights reserved. No part of this book may be used or reproduced by any means, graphic, electronic, or mechanical, including photocopying, recording, taping or by any information storage retrieval system without the written permission of the authors.

Disclaimer

This book is a work of fiction. Names, characters, places, and incidents are products of the authors' imagination or are used fictitiously and are not to be construed as real. Any resemblance to actual events, locales, organizations, or people, living or dead, is entirely coincidental.

Cover Design by Cameron Kamenicky and Naomi Lucas
Edited by Lindsay York at LY Publishing Services

Created with Vellum

# CHAPTER ONE

Mariah pulled her beat-up old Camaro into the parking lot for the city park and let it shudder to a halt. She clenched the steering wheel in an attempt to keep her hands from trembling. *Too much caffeine*, she tried to tell herself. But even though she'd been guzzling coffee all night, she knew that wasn't the reason she was shaking.

Forcing her hands to release the wheel, she reached for the small bouquet of flowers sitting on the passenger seat. They weren't much—just a cheap bouquet from the last gas station—but she had wanted to bring something, some token to acknowledge that this was the last place where her sister Judith and her nephew Charlie had been seen.

As she climbed out of her car, her collection of bracelets jingled, the sound startling in the still morning air. With a muttered curse, she pulled off all but the frayed friendship bracelet her sister had tied around her wrist not five days before she disappeared. Judith had laughed and tugged one of the braids scattered throughout Mariah's long blond hair as she displayed her own bracelet.

"There. Is that hippie enough for you?"

Mariah's eyes filled with tears as she remembered that morning in her sister's small townhouse, as neat and organized as her sister. Why hadn't she stayed with her for just a few more days? But she had already been restless, the same restlessness that had kept her on the road for more than fifteen years pulling at her. Despite the joy of spending time with her sister and her new nephew, she'd left that day for a gig in Detroit. The police had contacted her a week later.

Now she took a deep breath, wiped her eyes, and turned towards the park. Even though the summer sun hadn't yet crept above the horizon, the parking lot wasn't entirely deserted. A big black Escalade stood guard at one end and two mom vans were parked by the walking trail. Mariah gave them a wistful glance as she passed by, noting the car seats and the colorful assortment of toys. Judith had a similar model, still sitting in her townhouse driveway. Mariah hadn't been able to bring herself to sell it.

The path led into the woods, still cool and dim in the dawn light. Her sandals made no sound on the asphalt and nothing disturbed the hush that lay over the park. She started to hum, but the sound was so unnerving that she stopped and focused on reaching her destination instead. Around the next curve, a meadow opened up, leading down to a small lake with a bandstand perched on the shore. That was where the police had found the jogging stroller.

As she emerged into the meadow, she paused. Mist drifted up from the water, obscuring most of the open area, and the same unnatural quiet persisted. A breeze whispered past, like cool fingers against her skin, and she shivered. The mist cleared for a fraction of a second and... what was that? Her heart started to pound.

All her life, she had been addicted to stories of the supernatural, of the unusual, and that included UFOs. She had no doubt about what she had seen in that quick glimpse. A huge spaceship, gleaming in dark metal, hovered over one end of the meadow with a ramp descending to the ground. No wonder the police had never found any trace of Judith or Charlie.

Straining to see through the mist, she moved closer. Her heart was pounding so hard she felt sick but a spaceship here in the same place, exactly one year later? It had to be the same aliens. And maybe, just maybe, there was a chance that her sister and her nephew weren't lost to her forever.

A slight rustle penetrated the fog-muffled air and she dropped down into the long grass lining the shore, not caring that the wet grass instantly dampened her long skirt and peasant blouse. A man appeared, dressed in a severe black suit and facing away from her. She started to call out, to warn him, but then he raised his hand and her mouth went dry. It was not a human hand. Six long fingers, impossibly smooth and white, manipulated something that looked oddly like a radar detector.

He scanned the area but just as he turned in her direction, a low call sounded from behind him. A second man—no, a second alien—appeared and they had a brief conversation in a clicking language. Her pulse racing, she automatically reached for her phone, but it was completely dead, not even a flicker of light appearing despite what she knew had been a full charge.

While she was trying to decide what to do, two more aliens came down the ramp. Three of them disappeared off into the mist, while the fourth one stayed behind, examining a tablet-like screen with a disinterested air.

*Probably checking alien Facebook*, she thought half-hysterically. If he would just move a little farther away, she might be able to sneak onto the ramp behind him. Wait a minute. Was she seriously going to try and sneak aboard? Even as she wondered, she knew the answer was yes. She twisted her bracelet ruefully. Her sister would have been the first one to tell her she was being impulsive and reckless, but Judith and Charlie were her only family. If there was even a small chance that she could find them, she was going to take that chance.

The alien wandered a little farther away, still focused on his screen, and she crouched on the balls of her feet, ready to make a dash for it. A startled cry came from the far end of the meadow and then the unmistakable sound of a gunshot. The alien took off at a run in that direction.

Mariah paused for just a second to make sure no one else was coming, then took a deep breath and darted up the long metal ramp, her heart thudding against her ribs.

Inside, she found a dim, cavernous space more than half-filled with a wide variety of containers, some of them resembling huge packing crates much taller than her, while others were stacks of what looked like Tupperware boxes. All of them were strapped into place in some complicated arrangement that she didn't quite understand. Based on every science fiction movie she had ever watched, this must be the cargo hold.

She immediately ducked down one of the narrow pathways between the containers, anxious to get out of sight in case someone else appeared. Should she stay here? There didn't appear to be anyone else around and there were a number of little nooks and crannies where she could hide. But then she remembered that even on an Earth plane, the cargo area was unheated and unpressurized. In the case of a spaceship, it might not even have oxygen.

Biting her lip and trying to keep her damp sandals from squeaking on the metal floor, she sidled back behind the stacks, then edged along the white metal wall until she came to a door panel. No one had appeared, so she took a deep breath and pressed the button next to the door. With a soft whoosh, the door slid open to reveal an empty white corridor and a whiff of antiseptic air. As soon as she passed through the opening, the door slid shut behind her and she had to suppress a surge of panic. There was nowhere to hide in the open hallway, and she needed to find somewhere where she could conceal herself as soon as possible. One side of the passageway was lined with half a dozen door panels, while the other side held only two. Did that mean that they opened into larger areas, with more room to hide? Or were they just more likely to be populated?

Shuddering at the thought of opening a door to a sea of alien faces, she opted for the first of the six doors. Crossing her fingers that her assumption was correct, she tentatively pressed the button next to the door. A small storage room met her gaze, but the walls were lined with floor-to-ceiling cabinets and there was nowhere to hide. Her heart thudded and sweat began to dampen her palms as she moved to the next door and she had to force herself to press the open button. This looked like a better option. It resembled a small lab, with a counter along one side that included something resembling a sink, and rows of tall shelves perpendicular to the counter on the other. She thought she could conceal herself between the shelves and as she looked at the sink, it occurred to her that she would be able to at least have something to drink.

The practical thought of food and drink brought her to a sudden stop. What the hell was she thinking? She didn't have any supplies; she didn't have a plan. All she had was a desperate hope that this ship, appearing in the same place where her sister and nephew had disappeared exactly a year earlier could somehow lead her to them. She took a deep breath and squared her shoulders.

Yes, it was foolish, it was reckless, but they were the only two people in the world who she loved, and she was going to take this chance.

Her resolve was tested almost immediately when she heard

voices in the corridor. In a cold sweat, she rushed to the rear of the room and wedged herself behind the last set of shelves. It was a tight fit, but no one would be able to see her unless they were standing directly in front of her. A second later, she heard the door panel open.

## CHAPTER TWO

As Mariah heard the door open, she slid down the wall of her hiding place as quietly as she could until she was huddled in a small heap. Her heart sank as at least two voices filled the small room, the clicking sounds of their language reminding her uneasily of insect noises. From the increased volume and rapid exchange, she suspected they were having an argument.

*Great.* The last thing she wanted was to be discovered by aliens who were already angry.

As if in response to her thoughts, a figure appeared at the end of the shelves bordering her hiding place. She peeked up over her bent knees, praying that he would not look in her direction. Like the aliens she had seen outside the ship, he was tall and thin with flat white skin and matte black hair. The severe black outfit she had mistaken for a suit appeared to be some type of uniform. He wasn't looking in her direction. Instead, he was waving his hand at his unseen companion. His six-fingered hand, she noted again, and for some reason that difference more than any other drove home to her just how alien these beings were and sent a shudder up her spine.

The alien made a frustrated gesture, then she watched in slow-motion horror as he turned until his glowing red eyes looked directly at her. His eyes widened as she froze, too afraid to move. She braced herself for his outraged cry or for a weapon to appear in his hand. Instead, he wiped his face blank of expression and turned back to his companion. His voice dropped to a soothing level and she could tell that the argument seemed to be coming to an end. A few moments later, she heard the door panel open again.

What had happened? She knew that he had seen her—his reaction had been quite obvious. A horrible possibility occurred to her. What if he intended to go and get more of the aliens? After a moment's thought, she decided that didn't seem likely. While he was definitely slender, he was easily a head taller and she suspected he would have little trouble subduing her. Whatever his reasons, what mattered now was finding a new place to hide while he was gone.

As she pushed herself upright, she realized to her horror that he hadn't left after all. Once again, he stood at the entrance to her little hideaway. She braced herself, prepared to fight even if the effort proved futile, but he merely stood there and looked at her. She stared back, waiting for him to take some action but he didn't move. Eventually the tension proved too much for her.

"What are you going to do to me?" she whispered, then groaned inwardly. It was a silly question, but it was all she could think to say.

He regarded her thoughtfully for another moment, then disappeared. Had she chased him off?

Before she had a chance to feel relieved, he reappeared and this time he had a long silver syringe in his hand.

"No! No, I won't let you."

She scrabbled frantically at the wall behind her, trying to get away from the threat of the needle even though she had nowhere to go. The shelves next to her contained a variety of boxes and jars and she slid her hand across them as discreetly as possible, trying to find something she could use as a weapon. The alien made what looked like a gesture for her to calm down, patting the air in front of him.

"No! I'm not going to relax. I won't let you stick that thing in me."

Her voice rose as she spoke and this time, he cast a quick look over his shoulder and then pressed a hand to his mouth. He wanted her to be quiet? But why?

The obvious answer was that he didn't want anyone else to know that she was here, but she couldn't decide if that was an advantage or a disadvantage. Did he just not want to share her with the rest of the crew? Even though that was a horrible thought, a single alien would no doubt be easier to handle than a group of them. And at least so far, he had done nothing threatening, although she still eyed the syringe with suspicion.

"What is that for?" she asked in a much quieter voice.

He pointed to his mouth and then to his ear, then pointed at her and repeated the gesture.

"Do you mean you want to talk to me?" It was the only way she could interpret his gestures, although she had no idea how a shot would help her understand.

He nodded and took a step forward.

"No!" she cried again, trying to press back against the wall.

He stopped immediately, casting another nervous look over his shoulder and pressed his hand to his mouth again. He obviously did not want anyone else to overhear her, and that was a good thing, right? She remembered her earlier fear of being surrounded by a sea of alien faces as every sci-fi horror movie she had ever seen flashed through her mind.

Taking a deep breath, she did her best to keep her voice low and reasonable. "That thing you're holding, are you saying it will help me understand you?"

He nodded eagerly. The fact that he seemed to understand English was both alarming and encouraging. Obviously, he had encountered humans before, and what if he even knew something about her sister? That hope was enough to make her gingerly move away from the wall.

"Are you going to hurt me?"

He hesitated, then nodded his head. Holding up one hand, he unclenched two fingers, with a brief pause between each. Hopefully that meant the pain would not last longer than it took him to display his fingers. Straightening her shoulders, she stepped forward. How Judith would have laughed to see her voluntarily taking a shot. Throughout her childhood, she had fought her sister every time she had needed any type of inoculation. *This is for you, Ju*, she thought as she held out her arm.

Instead of taking her outstretched arm, the alien clamped his fingers on her shoulder—long, cold, surprisingly strong fingers. Before she could object, he raised the syringe to her neck and there was a brief flare of agony as an icy cold current raced through her body.

"Ow!" she cried, but she remembered to keep her voice low.

"I am sorry for the pain that I caused," the alien said apologetically, and she gaped at him. She could understand him perfectly. "I am afraid that less painful methods of inserting a translation implant are not available on a Vedeckian ship."

Trying to wrap her mind around the fact that she was actually talking to an alien, she rubbed the place where he had inserted the syringe. As he had promised, the sting was already fading.

"A Vedeckian ship? Is that what we are on?" she asked uncertainly.

"Yes, it is, and I need to get you off of it as soon as possible." He tilted his head, red eyes glowing. "Why did you choose to come onboard? Did you not realize that the ship was not native to your planet?"

"Of course I knew that the ship didn't belong on Earth. But unless I'm wrong—" *how she prayed she was not wrong* "—a ship like this took my sister and my nephew away last year."

"You are searching for your kin?" He stepped back with an appalled look on his face. "You must know that is not possible."

"Why isn't it possible?"

He shook his head. "You must leave the ship now. I could possibly find out about your kin, but..."

A low, penetrating hum filled the room. Her new companion seemed to sag.

"I'm afraid it is too late. We are leaving."

"Good," she said fiercely, even though her stomach cramped with anxiety. She had made it this far; she wasn't going to let anything else deter her.

"You do not understand. This is a slave ship. Commander Kadica is taking the females on this vessel to be sold at auction."

Now it was her turn to sag as she stared at him in horror.

"You mean Judith? Charlie? They were sold as slaves?"

What had these aliens done to her family?

Forcing back her tears, she scowled at the male in front of her. "Why are you even trying to be nice to me? And why did you try and get me to leave? I would have thought you wanted more prisoners."

"*I* don't want any prisoners." He hesitated, casting another look around the small room as if checking to make sure that no one had snuck up on them. He lowered his voice until she could barely hear him. "I am working to stop the slave trade."

"Stop it?" In her excitement, she stepped forward and grabbed his arm. He flinched and ducked back but she was too excited to wonder about his actions. "Does that mean you could help me find my sister and get her free?"

"I am afraid it is not quite that simple. First of all, we would need to find out where she was sold." He stopped, suddenly looking thoughtful. "Your sister, was she like you?"

*Not at all*, she started to reply and then realized he was probably asking about physical appearance rather than personality. "Yes, I guess so."

They both had pale blonde hair, although Judith kept hers in a neat short bob whereas Mariah's long hair was currently decorated with tiny braids and pink highlights. They were of a similar height and build as well and both of them had inherited their father's blue eyes.

"There was a female with a male child taken on the previous journey to this planet. She was only transferred to our ship for a brief period before Commander Khaen made other arrangements."

"Other arrangements? What other arrangements?"

He shook his head. "I do not know. I was a new crew member at the time and he neither liked nor trusted me. I suspect it was a private transaction."

"Is there any way you can ask this Commander Khaen?"

Her heart sank as he shook his head again. "I am afraid not. Commander Khaen is dead."

"What about his records?" she asked desperately. "Surely he must have kept some type of records."

"Perhaps. He was not a… pleasant individual and he did not trust anyone. But we have been able to track some of his activities."

"We?"

He ducked his head, looking suddenly embarrassed. "I have been working with a team on Trevelor to try and bring an end to the slave trade. It is the least I can do to make amends for some of the atrocities committed by my people."

"Can I speak to them?" She started to reach for his arm again but stopped herself. "I'm sure I can make them understand how important it is for me to find my sister and my nephew."

"You will have the opportunity." He sighed and pulled out a small device, opening the screen. "Once they receive my signal, they should intercept us within a few days. The plan was to return all of the captives to your planet with no memory of what had occurred."

"I can't go back, not now. Not now that I'm finally making some progress towards finding her."

"I will see what I can find out before then," he promised.

"Oh, thank you so much—uh, I'm sorry. I don't know your name."

"My name is Kwaret." He seemed cautiously pleased that she had asked.

"I'm Mariah." She smiled, full of excitement to finally have some hope after this long terrible year. "And you're like some undercover spy? Investigating the bad guys?"

Something that could almost have been a blush touched his white cheeks. "I suppose you could put it that way."

"But why? Why are you doing this?"

"I met another human female on my last trip to this planet and she treated me with a respect that I have never had from my own people. She made me realize that I had to try and put an end to something that I had always known was wrong but had never had the courage to prevent."

"That's wonderful. She sounds like an amazing woman. Did she get to go home?" she asked eagerly.

"No. She is now mated to a—"

A harsh buzz interrupted him, and he immediately started backing towards the door. "That is the assembly call. I cannot miss it. Stay here and do not try to leave the room. I will return as soon as I am able."

With surprising speed, he turned and disappeared. She heard the door panel close a moment later. A sudden torrent of relief and hope swept over her, her knees trembling now that she was alone. Once more she slid down the wall to her huddled position, buried her head in her knees, and burst into tears.

## CHAPTER THREE

Cestov Tok'Laren, Captain of the Confederated Planets Free Trader *Wanderer*, swore as he left his bridge. His small crew was usually quite competent despite their assorted backgrounds, but they had really fucked up this time. They were supposed to be transporting a cargo of rare pristidian seedlings—a perfect cargo, light, low maintenance, and extremely profitable. Somehow Maldost, his young assistant, had taken a slonga on board instead. The slonga was neither lightweight nor low maintenance and while it had the potential to be extremely valuable, it was illegal to transport outside of its home system. A system that was now two full days behind them. He headed for his cabin, tail whipping angrily, determined to try and find a place where they could sell the slonga—at a profit—before some nosy Confederated Planets Patrol ship approached them.

By the time he reached his cabin, some of his usual good humor had been restored. He had chosen this path. Unlike his brother, he had always been willing to play along the edges of the rules and this wasn't the first time he'd made a risky trade.

The thought of his brother caused the familiar pang. More than five years now and still he had found no trace of Bratan. Cestov had spent his time on Srashiman making inquiries instead of overseeing the trade. Now he was saddled with the slonga and still had no hint as to where he should look for his brother next.

"Damn you, Bratan. Why did you leave? You knew I didn't mean it," he muttered.

Pushing the painful memory aside, he sat down at his desk and brought up a map of the surrounding systems. Since the plague known as the Red Death had swept through the galaxy and devastated so many planets, a lot of the records in the ship's computer were outdated, but there were two nearby systems where he might be able to make the trade. The first was larger, but it was also more likely to be regulated. The other had only a single habitable planet, Trevelor, but it should be beyond the usual boundaries of the Patrol. The Patrol's numbers had also diminished as a result of the plague and they tended to concentrate on the central areas of the system, relying on volunteer craft farther out. He bent over the tablet, scrolling through the interweb message boards to review the latest information about Trevelor.

Halfway through his search, his heart rate increased. Several entries mentioned that Trevelor had become a haven for a variety of species because of the pleasant climate and the fact that they had been relatively untouched by the Red Death. One entry even mentioned a possible Cire colony.

Cestov was a Cire, one of the races most affected by the Red Death. The plague had been especially cruel to them. It had taken all of their women and their hope for the future. To the best of his knowledge, there were no longer any female Cires in existence. His tail flicked unhappily. He and his brother were the last generation that had been born before the plague and their father had taken them from Ciresia not long after their mother died. The older male had never been the same after her death, but he had lived long enough to make sure that both boys were prepared to take over the *Wanderer* and support themselves. Of course, their father had assumed that they would do it together. For the first ten years after his death, they had done just that, but five years ago they had a bitter argument and when he woke the next morning, his brother was gone. If only he could go back in time and take back the things he had said.

He shook his head. There was no use dwelling on something he couldn't change. All he could do was to keep searching for his brother and in this case, thankfully, it looked like his search and his business would coincide. They were headed for Trevelor.

"Captain!" Maldost burst into his cabin with an excited look on his face.

"Now what?"

"The slonga is giving birth!"

"What the hell do you mean it's giving birth? First, you tell me that you traded for a slonga instead of the seedlings you were supposed to obtain and now you're telling me that the creature is female?"

The anger in his voice finally penetrated the young crew member's excitement, and he bowed his head, his ears flicking down in apology. Maldost was an Afbera, another race to lose many of their females to the plague, although not to the extent of the Cire. Perhaps that was why Maldost did not understand the appalling act he had propagated. The female was now separated from her mate and was about to have young without any assistance or anything familiar surrounding her.

"I didn't know that she was female," Maldost protested.

"Just that the slonga was trapped in a too-small cage. And that it was worth a lot of credits," he added hastily.

Cestov sighed and rubbed his head, a headache already forming beneath his lamella, the ridges on his scalp which marked his age and warrior status.

"Can you tell if she is in distress?" Not that either one of them had any experience with females—of any kind—in labor.

"Well, she is making a sort of grunting noise?"

"All right. Let's go see what we can do to ease this birth. Did you summon Whovian?"

Maldost scowled, his fangs showing. "He said he was a medic, not a veterinarian. And he smelled like liquor again."

Cestov's tail twitched angrily as he and Maldost took off for the cargo bay at a run. He had known when he took the medic on board that Whovian had been running from some kind of trouble, but he hadn't realized that the trouble had been of the male's own making. The drunken idiot was leaving the ship at the next port. Twice now he had been softhearted enough to believe the male's promises of improved behavior. The third time was enough.

He was still scowling at the male's absence when they reached the slonga. A low grunting could be heard from the entrance to the cargo area and he looked down to see big dark eyes fastened on him, as if imploring him for assistance. Fuck. He had no experience and no equipment, but he could not resist that look of entreaty.

He pushed up his sleeves as he strode across the room.

"Start searching the interwebs to see if you can find any information," he ordered Maldost.

"There, there," he said soothingly as he stroked the slonga's long pink fur, trying his best to sound calm and confident. The slonga mooed and wrapped her trunk around his arm. Still murmuring gently to her, he stroked the large mound of her stomach. How could they not have realized that she might be with young?

She grunted again, and he saw the very tip of a tiny trunk appear between her back set of legs. Prepared or not, she was giving birth and he was the only one here to help her.

Two hours later, Cestov sat back with a weary smile. Three tiny slonga calves snuggled against their mother as they nursed happily. But then he realized that the last one, the smallest one, had been pushed to one side and wasn't moving.

"Maldost, did you find anything about an infant who isn't moving?" he asked urgently.

Instinctively, he picked up the tiny creature and started rubbing the small sides. The mother mooed again, her trunk reaching for the infant.

"When they came out, she rubbed all of them with her trunk," Maldost said anxiously. "Like you're doing, but it looked much harder."

He started stroking the calf again, more firmly this time, but there was still no response. Frantically searching for a solution, he finally remembered a technique his father had mentioned a long time ago when he was teaching them basic medical skills. He bent down over the infant and began gently compressing its ribs while he breathed into the tiny mouth. For an agonizing few minutes, nothing happened but then he finally felt a small movement, and a minute later the tiny trunk wrapped around his wrist. His tail circled the much smaller length protectively as he sighed with relief. Too many things had been lost to death over the past generation—people, planets, family—but he had managed to save one small life.

He helped the calf begin nursing, delighted when she latched on and began to drink, first slowly, then with surprising eagerness. When he looked up, Maldost was grinning at him and he couldn't resist grinning back before he hardened his expression.

"You are very lucky that I managed to save her. If she had died, it would have been on your head."

Maldost's ears went down and he whined softly at the reprimand. Since Cestov knew that it was thoughtlessness rather than cruelty that had driven the younger male's behavior, he relented slightly.

"And you will make up for it, by ensuring that this bedding is kept fresh and clean." Even as he spoke, one of the infants wandered far enough away from his mother to let loose a gushing yellow flow. How could such a small creature produce so much shit? Maldost winced and nodded.

"I will take care of them," he promised.

Cestov started to rise to his feet, only to be stopped by the slonga's trunk wrapping around his arm. He looked at the big dark eyes watching him so intently. The slonga were known for their intelligence, but no one had ever suggested that they were sentient. The look of gratitude in the creature's eyes contradicted that.

"You'll be all right. You and your calves," he said softly.

Before he could start to leave again, he felt a small weight against his knee. The youngest calf had finished feeding and curled up against him. His tail immediately covered it. The rest of the infants were tucked against the mother's stomach but this one had come to him. With a sigh, he settled back down. It appeared that he would be spending the night down here.

## CHAPTER FOUR

Mariah paced restlessly. The week had dragged on with agonizing boredom interrupted by a few moments of sheer terror. Even though there was a slight risk of others entering the small lab, Kwaret had decided that she was safer here than anywhere else on the ship. He had done everything he could to ensure her comfort in her small hiding place, but she'd still been lonely and bored. Too scared even to sing, she'd only emerged once the ship was deep in the night shift to work through some yoga poses and wash using the sink.

On her second day in hiding, two strange Vedeckians had entered the room. Fortunately, she had been obediently tucked away in her little hidey-hole, although she doubted that it would endure a full scrutiny. Kwaret had arranged a stack of containers at the end of the shelving unit but they were empty and easily pushed aside. She held her breath, frozen in place as she listened to their conversation.

"Hurry up. You know we're not supposed to be in here," the first speaker said urgently.

A sneering laugh made her skin crawl.

"Who's going to say anything—that spineless worm? I don't even know why Kadica took him on."

"He serves a purpose. And he gets the smallest share."

Bottles clinked and she moved a fraction closer, trying to catch a glimpse of what they were doing through a crack in the containers.

"Three females and two infants. A small reward for the risk."

The speaker had his back to her, but she could see him combining the contents of several bottles.

The other male shrugged. "Not that much risk. And not that small a reward. Last year's pickup was most profitable and this year we can keep all of them. We don't have to give up anyone to Commander Khaen. A breeder and two infants, just because he found this planet? Ridiculous."

Her pulse increased and she edged a little closer. Could they possibly be talking about Judith and Charlie?

"We don't have to pay him because he disappeared." The first male looked up and frowned. "How can you say no risk?"

"No risk on this primitive planet. No alarms, no one waiting. I say it's been a successful test. I will suggest to the commander that we increase the frequency of our visits and expand our search area."

"I would feel more comfortable if we knew why Commander Khaen disappeared after last year's visit."

"Probably ran into the Patrol." The second male shrugged again. "No one's come after us, have they? Stop worrying."

The male at the counter turned and held up a vial of green fluid. He grinned, pointed teeth flashing. "This should help."

"Are you sure? It looks toxic."

"Only toxic enough to make me stop worrying. Let's go."

They had departed without even approaching her hiding place, but her heart hadn't stopped pounding for a long time.

A few days later, her anxiety flared again when Kwaret didn't make his usual visit. He tried to come twice a day, once in the morning and once in the evening, but when he missed the evening visit, she was not too concerned. She had heard the assembly alarm and assumed he had been required to attend. When he did not appear the next morning either, her concern started to grow.

What was she going to do without his assistance? She still had a reasonable quantity of the tasteless nutrition bars he had provided, and she could always get water from the sink. Her other bodily needs were resolved by the use of the waste incinerator. She should be able to survive if he didn't return. She might even be able to find a way off the ship if they landed or were intercepted, although it would undoubtedly be an easier process if Kwaret was able to assist her. But practical concerns aside, she was also worried about the alien male. During their conversations, she had come to respect and even like him. He had a gentle deference that seemed at odds with the information he somewhat reluctantly shared about his people and a dry sense of humor that emerged as he grew more comfortable in her presence.

By the time the second evening approached, she was pacing the small room anxiously. When she heard the door panel start to open, she made a dive for her hiding place.

"You should be more careful. What if I had been someone else?" Kwaret's voice was so hoarse it was almost unrecognizable.

She whirled thankfully to greet him and stopped with a horrified gasp. He had quite obviously been beaten. One eye was swollen half shut, a livid bruise darkened the white skin across his cheekbone, and one wrist was in a bandage.

"What happened?"

He sighed wearily, then gingerly sat in the small chair he

had brought into the room. It was the only time he had ever sat in her presence.

"There was an issue with one of the captives. I tried to intervene, but I think I caused more harm than good."

Damn. A pang of guilt swept through her. She had been so busy thinking about her sister and nephew, and how she was going to find them and how she was going to get them back to Earth, that she hadn't stopped to consider the other women and children on board. Kwaret had assured her that they would be returned to Earth as soon as they were intercepted, and she had dismissed them from her mind.

"What sort of an issue?"

He shook his head, looking both baffled and oddly admiring.

"One of the females—the single female without a child—convinced the other two females to try and escape. They attacked Kragan when he brought food."

"Oh my goodness. I assume they didn't succeed?"

"They succeeded well enough to have him open the cell."

"But what were they going to do then? I doubt any of us could drive the ship."

The admiring look grew stronger. "Jade, the female behind all this, pointed his own weapon at Kragan. She demanded that the ship turn around or she would shoot him."

Mariah laughed at the image, then sobered rapidly. Obviously, it had not ended well. "What happened?"

"She underestimated the value that Commander Kadica puts on the lives of his crew members. He shot the male. He was going to shoot her as well when I tried to intervene."

"Oh no. Did he shoot her?"

Kwaret winced. "No. I managed to remind him that she was a valuable product. This is the result of my audacity."

"I'm so sorry. And the woman? What happened to her?"

"She has been fitted with a shock collar." Sadness crossed Kwaret's face. "She did not take it well and tried to fight. She is now unconscious."

Mariah found herself admiring the other woman's bravery, even as she shuddered at the story. She suspected that she would not have had the same courage.

"And the other women?"

"They ceased all resistance as soon as the male was shot."

"They didn't stand up for her?" she asked indignantly.

"It would have been a useless effort, and they had infants to protect."

Silence fell over the small room and Kwaret leaned back in his chair with his eyes closed.

"Why are you doing this? Not you personally I mean, but your people," she finally blurted out. She had been thinking about the situation over the past few days and it seemed like a lot of effort to go to another planet just to abduct a few women and children.

"Vedeck is one of a number of star systems that fall under the leadership of the Confederated Planets government. However, our entire civilization was severely damaged by a plague that raged for almost twenty years before it was brought under control. The plague took billions and billions of lives, but females suffered the worst. Now we have a number of systems that are short on females and therefore on children. There are many desperate people who are willing to do whatever it takes to find a mate, to have a child."

She stared at him in stunned horror, as she tried to wrap her mind around the idea that so many individuals had fallen prey to this disease.

"And your government allows this? Permits stealing women and children?"

"Absolutely not—that is, if you are referring to the Confederated Planets government. If… *when* we are intercepted, everyone on board will be imprisoned for life." He sighed and slumped down in the chair, looking defeated. "But my people, the Vedeckians, are more concerned with profit than with rules. There was a preliminary expedition last year. Three commanders volunteered. I served under Commander Khaen, who was the leader of the group. I know he demanded tribute from the other commanders, and I believe that your sister and nephew, along with another child, were his tribute from Commander Kadica."

"And you said Commander Khaen is dead?"

"Yes. We were intercepted by a Cire ship and taken into custody. Commander Khaen made an unsuccessful attempt to overtake that ship and perished. But I wanted to bring an end to the entire business. I managed to work my way onto this ship in anticipation that they would try again and that I would be able to shut them down as well."

"What about the third commander?"

He started to shrug, then winced. "No one knows. He has not been heard from since then."

"The two that were in here a few days ago, they said this was a trial. That there would be more." Dread filled her at the thought of more innocent women and children being taken by these aliens to be sold. While she could sympathize with what must be a number of desperate races, there was no justification for stealing other individuals.

"Yes, that is why the ship needs to be intercepted and prevented from returning to Vedeck."

"Earlier, you said *if* we were intercepted," she said slowly.

He avoided her gaze for a long moment, then finally sighed.

"I have a transmitter that I was to use to alert the Cire ship if this occurred again. They are supposed to be monitoring for the signal, but I am concerned because I have not received a response. It has been many months since I was taken into this crew. I hope they have not stopped waiting for my signal."

Her heart skipped a beat. "What if they have? How am I going to find Judith and Charlie?" The other problem struck her as she spoke. "And what's going to happen to me?"

"I will protect you to the best of my ability," he promised. "We are currently headed to Driguera. There is a port there with a somewhat... questionable reputation. Commander Kadica plans to auction off the troublesome female."

"You can't let him do that!"

"I know. If I can't reach my contacts, I will have no choice but to call in the Patrol." He did not seem happy about the idea.

"Is that bad?"

"They will arrest the entire crew and I doubt that I will gain much leniency because I called them." He squinted at her with his working eye. "And they will erase the memories of all of the humans and return them to Earth. Including you."

## CHAPTER FIVE

"But Captain..." Maldost whined as he trailed reluctantly behind Cestov through the crowded streets of the underground market on Driguera.

"Stop complaining. You knew when you brought the slonga on board that she required specific nutrients."

"I did. And I thought I had secured enough supplies."

"Just like you thought that she was a male?" he said dryly.

Maldost's ears went down. "You're never going to let me forget that, are you?"

"No. Which is one of the reasons that you are buying supplies using your own credits."

They both knew that Cestov would never let the slonga or her calves starve, but he intended this as a lesson for the younger male. He had already arranged to have his navigator procure additional bedding.

Maldost followed him in abashed silence as they turned down a narrow alley lined with a variety of food stalls. The aromas were overwhelming, ranging from tantalizing to unspeakably foul. The stalls were stacked high with skewers of unidentifiable fried substances, fruits of every description, piles of baked goods, and hundreds of other types of food. A cacophony of voices hawked their wares. As usual, his crew member bounced back quickly from the reprimand.

"We should stop and have a meal while we're here," Maldost suggested hopefully, casting a longing gaze at a stall selling strips of some kind of dried meat.

Cestov sighed. "Maldost, this is not a recreational trip. We need to get the supplies, get back to the *Wanderer*, and get off Driguera. The last thing we need is for the Patrol to decide to make one of their periodic raids on this place while we have the slonga on board."

"We could just get something to take with us—"

"I beg your pardon, sir. May I have a word?"

Cestov scowled at the Vedeckian addressing him. The tall white-skinned male was a member of a species he despised with all his heart. They called themselves traders also, but they had no scruples and gave the entire profession a bad name. The male was accompanied by a small figure completely covered in a dark cloak and he wondered who had been unlucky enough to fall into the Vedeckian's clutches.

"I have no time for you, Vedeckian," he growled and started to move on.

To his shock, the male had the audacity to grab his arm. He snatched the Vedeckian's hand, squeezing the narrow bones together.

"You forget yourself."

He heard a soft gasp from the cloaked figure and something about the sound caught his attention but before he could investigate, his captive spoke again.

"Please, sir. You must listen—I need you to call for assistance from another Cire ship."

"You want me to call a Cire ship?" The unexpected request

made him drop the male's hand. Most of his people had remained on Ciresia despite the plague. Could his brother simply have moved on to another ship? And yet... "You know we have no use for your kind."

"I have been working with other Cires to stop an illegal trade operation," the Vedeckian lowered his voice to a barely perceptible whisper, "transporting females."

He stepped back, stunned and disgusted by the very idea. To treat a precious female as an object to be bought and sold? Maldost growled, a low rumbling sound that echoed his own anger, and another soft noise came from the cloaked figure.

"Why should I believe you?" He frowned suspiciously at the other male.

"I know you have no reason to do so, but there are females who need assistance and you are my only hope unless I call in the Patrol."

This was exactly the type of quixotic quest that would appeal to his brother.

"What is the name of the Cire captain?" he demanded.

"The former captain was Hrebec Nak'Charen, but he has retired on Trevelor."

Another mention of the planet. If the captain had retired there, it was even more likely that a Cire colony existed. He tried to suppress the surge of hope. It would not be the first time he had been disappointed.

"And the current captain?"

"Captain Armad? He is not Cire, but a large part of the crew is still of your race. Will you help me?"

He had every intention of contacting the ship to see if his brother was on board, but to request aid for the Vedeckian? A part of him wanted to shrug and tell him to call in the authorities, but how could he know if the Vedeckian would actually take such a step? He also had a measure of sympathy for the male's reluctance to call in the Patrol. While they did an excellent job of enforcing law and order, they tended to see every situation in black and white and rarely considered any nuances. It didn't help matters that he would also be in trouble if they arrived before he could exit the port.

"What exactly do you want me to do?" he asked.

"Could we perhaps find somewhere less crowded to discuss the matter?" The Vedeckian cast a nervous glance around the crowded street.

Perhaps he had a point. They had not yet attracted a crowd, but more than one interested glance had been sent in their direction.

"Very well. Maldost, it appears you are going to get your wish after all. We will use one of the upstairs rooms at the Tavern of the Four Winds." He turned back to the Vedeckian. "You know the place?"

"Yes, but we must hurry."

That soft sound caught his attention again and he looked down to see that his tail was tugging gently at the cloak of the Vedeckian's companion. What the hell? He sternly brought it back under control, resisting the impulse to apologize.

"Lead the way. We will follow a step or two behind."

The Vedeckian gave an abrupt nod and he and his companion moved up the street. Cestov felt an odd reluctance to let the cloaked figure out of his sight and he followed perhaps less discreetly than was advisable, even as his excitement increased. Two possible leads on his brother—this was more than he'd had in years.

"Captain, what are you doing?" Maldost asked. "You don't really trust that male, do you? You know you can't trust a Vedeckian."

"Normally, I would agree with you, but he seemed... different. I believe that he is sincere. And what reason would he have to lie?" The tall figure ahead of them moved with surprising speed and Cestov increased his pace, still unwilling to let the cloaked figure get too far away. "And if he is telling the truth, I am honor-bound to help."

"Well, yes, of course." Maldost lowered his voice. "You don't really think they are trading in females, do you?"

"Would you put anything past the Vedeckians?" he asked grimly.

The male and his companion disappeared into the tavern and he increased his speed again. At least the male had had the sense to choose the rear entry. He ducked through the same door just as the host, a portly Drigueran, came back down the stairs.

"I am expected," he said shortly.

"Yes, of course. However, you do understand there is a fee for the discretion of the house?" The Drigueran leered at him and Cestov couldn't help wondering exactly what he thought was going to occur in the upstairs room.

He handed over a small amount of credits, then a second handful. "Bring us two meals and two mugs of ale as well."

The Drigueran looked at the credits and his eyes turned greedy but then he took another look at the two of them and simply bowed his head. "I will make the arrangements. Top of the stairs, third door on the right."

Unexpectedly eager, Cestov took the stairs two at a time. The dingy hallway did not look promising, but he had been here before and knew that the private dining rooms were more luxurious than one would expect.

Now that they were away from the street and the constant bombardment of food odors, he caught a tantalizing hint of fragrance, something delicate and floral that he had never encountered before. He wondered if he would be able to discover the source once his meeting was concluded, but as he pushed open the third door, he realized that the delightful scent had increased.

As he expected, the room was lushly decorated with heavily carved wall panels in dark crimson and matching padded benches surrounding a low central table, but his attention focused on the Vedeckian and his cloaked companion. He caught a hint of a soft voice as the concealed figure whispered urgently to the other male and he instinctively drew closer.

As soon as he was within arm's reach, his tail once again tugged at the cloak before he could stop it.

"Would you stop doing that?"

The low soft voice was unquestionably feminine, and he stared in bemused wonder as she threw back the hood of her cloak. A mass of long pale hair tumbled out and big blue eyes stared up at him indignantly. Pale golden skin, completely defenseless, covered a soft round face with a funny little nose and an impossibly lush pink mouth. All of the blood in his body went straight to his shaft.

## CHAPTER SIX

Mariah stared up at the big alien whose tail—his *tail*—had been tugging at her cloak. She had never imagined anyone remotely like him. Textured skin in shades of deep green covered almost reptilian features with a flat nose and a broad, thin mouth. Dark, wide-set eyes focused intently on her face. Instead of hair, he had darker ridges covering his head that continued down onto his shoulders—his very broad shoulders. The tight black shirt and pants he was wearing did nothing to conceal an extraordinarily impressive set of muscles. She should have been intimidated, but something about him instinctively made her feel safe.

"Damn, I've never seen anyone like you before."

The words came from her alien's companion and she reluctantly dragged her gaze away from him to look at the second male. He was as tall as her alien but completely different. His body was covered with light shaggy fur that thinned out over his face and hands, but he bore a distinct resemblance to some kind of bear. He had stepped forward eagerly as he spoke, and she shrank back as he extended a huge clawed hand towards her. Before she could object, her alien grabbed the bear's arm and snatched it back with a growl.

"Maldost, what the hell do you think you're doing?"

Maldost's ears went down and he whined, looking so abashed that her fear disappeared. He reminded her suddenly of a very large puppy.

"It's all right," she said. "I'm sure he didn't mean any harm."

His ears perked up, but her alien interrupted before he could speak.

"Perhaps not, but he does not understand how to behave around females."

"And you do?" The words popped out before she thought about what she was saying or how provocative they would sound. It didn't help that her voice had gone low and husky.

"I know to treat them with great care," he said solemnly, but there was a heat in his gaze that caused an answering stir in her own body as she had a sudden image of exactly what type of care she wanted from him.

What in the world was wrong with her? She forced herself to look at Kwaret instead. This was his plan, after all.

THEY HAD LANDED IN THE PORT ONLY A FEW HOURS AGO. Kwaret had still not received an answer to his signal and was grimly considering calling the Patrol. He left her in the lab while he went to check and see if the route off the ship was clear. He came hurrying back a few minutes later.

"A trader just landed, and I saw the captain get off the ship. He is a Cire."

"What does that mean?" she asked as she watched him rummage through one of the drawers.

"I am working with members of their race—they are the

ones who are waiting for my signal. Perhaps he can get a message to them. Here, put this on."

He handed her a long dark cloak with a hood and she frowned at him even as she obeyed and pulled it over her clothing.

"Why am I putting this on?"

"Because I'm going to take you off the ship with me. This is the perfect time. Everyone not on guard duty has already disbursed."

"What? Why?" Hurt and betrayal filled her voice. Was he going to abandon her here?

"I hope that if the Cire can make contact with the ship with which I am working, they can take you to Trevelor. They have all the records we were able to recover from Commander Khaen."

Part of her was excited that she might be one step closer to finding Judith and Charlie, but she dreaded the thought of leaving Kwaret. She had grown to trust him over the past week, and she was not at all sure about leaving his protection.

"Are you sure you can trust him?"

"The Cire have a strong reputation for honor and responsibility." Sadness washed across his face. "Their race lost all their females to the Red Death."

"How horrible. Does that mean they are dying out?"

"Perhaps not. They have found that they are compatible with a few other races."

He gave her a speculative look, but before she could ask any additional questions, he told her to conceal herself in her hood. As soon as she was covered, he hurried her out the door and off the ship, moving at a pace that kept her at a jog.

When he stopped her alien in the food market, she had almost protested. The male and his companion made an intimidating display and she wasn't at all sure that she trusted them.

But then that curious tail tugged at her cloak in an oddly endearing gesture and she found her fear disappearing into amusement.

Now she realized that the tail was back, this time sliding around her wrist.

"Why are you doing this?" she asked, trying to sound indignant even though it felt strangely comforting. The surface of his tail was not smooth but covered in small nubs that teased her skin. Was he like that all over, she wondered, and darted a glance between his legs before she could stop herself. Oh my. He was apparently very pleased to meet her.

Her cheeks flushed pink and she hastily snatched her gaze away, but her nipples had tightened, and she could feel an ache low in her stomach. Flustered, she looked over to find Kwaret eyeing her with a strange expression on his face.

"As I mentioned before, we need your assistance," Kwaret said, turning back to her big alien.

"I am Captain Cestov Tok'Laren, at your service." He bowed deeply, his previous objections seemingly forgotten. "You said that you needed me to contact a ship?"

"Yes. My name is Kwaret and this is my... friend, Mariah."

He sounded so uncertain about using the term and she gave him a warm smile. Cestov made a noise that sounded suspiciously like a low growl, but Kwaret ignored it and continued.

"As I said, I have been working with a Cire ship, the *Defiance*. We are trying to prevent the Vedeckians from raiding the planet where Mariah is from to obtain females and infants. As a result of the most recent raid, there are three other females and two infants on our ship now."

Cestov snarled, showing a rather impressive set of teeth. What would those feel like nibbling on her neck, she wondered, feeling the color creep back into her cheeks.

"That is completely unacceptable," Cestov said.

Kwaret nodded. "I agree, however, I am but a single voice."

"We should rescue them," the young male said eagerly.

"I saw your ship," Kwaret said patiently. "It does not appear to be a military vessel. It will take superior force to convince Commander Kadica to back down. With my assistance, the *Defiance* can take the ship with minimal harm. Can you contact them?"

"I have every intention of doing so," Cestov said grimly. "How were you told to get in touch with them?"

The conversation turned technical and Mariah found herself watching Cestov as discreetly as possible. His face was so different from a human face and yet she had no difficulty in recognizing the expressions that flashed across it. Despite the intensity of the discussion, his gaze frequently flickered in her direction and his tail had once more come to rest on her, around her ankle this time. She didn't protest. It seemed harmless enough and the warm touch was curiously reassuring.

"Very well," Cestov concluded. "We will be on our way as soon as we have procured the supplies we need. And what of you?" He spoke to Kwaret, but he looked at her.

"I must remain in order to ensure the safety of the remaining females." Kwaret shook his head. "I am especially concerned about the troublesome female. I cannot let her be sold."

"Do you require our assistance to prevent it?"

Kwaret tilted his head as he considered the offer, then shook his head. "I have a plan. I think it would be best if you summon the ship as soon as possible. But there is one more thing."

"Yes?"

"I cannot protect all of the females and I do not believe that Mariah will be safe on my ship. Can you take her with you and arrange to have her transferred to the *Defiance*?"

## CHAPTER SEVEN

Take her with him? *Yes.* Cestov's body responded immediately and his tail tightened around her ankle. The thought of having her on the *Wanderer*, her delicate fragrance filling the air, her soft body so close—everything about it felt right. His cock had never really subsided and now it sprang back to a full aching erection at the idea of her at his side. But he did have another mission...

"I would be happy to take her, but I am headed for Trevelor," he said reluctantly. "I am searching for someone and unless he is on board the *Defiance*, I will simply pass along the message to them and continue to the planet."

"Trevelor?" Mariah interrupted. "But that's perfect. I'm also looking for someone and I hope that I can get some additional information there."

Before he could respond, there was a knock at the door. His hand immediately went to his blaster and he noted that Kwaret also had his hand on his weapon. Mariah paled and pulled her hood up over her head as he instinctively stepped in front of her. He nodded at Maldost to wait behind the door, then cautiously opened it.

The Drigueran stood outside, accompanied by a young male servant bearing two platters loaded with food while balancing two oversized mugs of ale.

"Your meal, sir," the host said obsequiously.

Without removing his hand from the hilt of his weapon, he gestured the servant inside. "Put everything on the table."

The young male nervously obeyed, keeping his head lowered. The Drigueran started to step inside the room as well, but Cestov blocked him. As soon as the servant scurried back past him, he shut the door in the innkeeper's face.

"I apologize," he said to Mariah. "When I ordered the food, I did not think to take your preferences into consideration. But please help yourself to anything that you would like."

He ignored Maldost's muffled protest. The young male would not be harmed by missing a meal and his instincts demanded that he feed his—*the* female first.

She still had not pushed her hood back down and he found himself impatient to see her face once more. As if in response to his desire, his tail once more tugged at the cloak. She laughed and he couldn't help but smile at the infectious sound. His admiration increased. She had been taken from her planet, surrounded by beings who were no doubt strange to her, but she had the courage and spirit to find humor in the situation.

"Please be seated," he urged.

"If you insist." She threw back the hood and this time she did not stop there but shrugged out of the cloak completely.

His mind ceased to function at the sight of soft lush curves barely contained by a Vedeckian uniform and all he could do was stare. He bit back his instinctive objection to the fact that she was obviously dressed in another male's clothing. The arms and legs had both been rolled up many, many times to accommodate her tiny frame, but despite her small size, everything about her was perfect. Before he could call it back, his tail wrapped around her waist. She jumped and blushed and he reluctantly brought his unruly tail back under control.

"Please sit down," he said again.

She looked a little uncertainly at Kwaret, then curled up on one of the low seats. He could no more have stopped himself from sitting next to her than he could have stopped himself from breathing. The Vedeckian and Maldost slid into place across from them.

"There are only two servings," she said softly. "This is your meal, isn't it?"

"We are delighted for you to have it. Aren't we, Maldost?"

His junior gave a somewhat reluctant nod and she laughed again.

"What if we all share it?"

"You will satisfy yourself first," he insisted.

"I don't really know what any of this is," she said with a rueful glance at the platters.

"Then I will assist you."

Despite his nosiness, the Drigueran had provided an excellent—and very large—meal. Cestov carefully chose small tidbits for Mariah, always checking to make sure that she enjoyed something before he urged her to take more. When it was apparent that she would eat no more than a small portion of the food, he indicated to Maldost that he could eat. The Vedeckian refused to partake, although he sipped the ale with an expression of pleasure on his white face.

Mariah also seemed to enjoy the ale, her face flushing a delicate pink and her laughter rippling frequently through the room. It wasn't until she leaned close to him and whispered confidentially in his ear that he realized she had become inebriated.

. . .

"You're very big," Mariah whispered to Cestov as she leaned closer to the big green alien.

Mmm, he smelled really good, like fall leaves and pumpkin spice. She leaned even closer, then yawned. That big arm looked like the perfect spot to rest her head. Surely, he wouldn't mind if she just rested her eyes for a minute. She let her head fall against his arm and his tail came up around her waist to support her. She patted it sleepily.

"That's a nice tail."

She could have sworn that she heard him moan but she felt too warm and comfortable and sleepy to worry about it. Her eyes closed and she nestled closer and for the first time since she had climbed aboard the alien ship, she felt truly safe.

The next thing Mariah remembered was waking up alone on a large bed. The mattress was soft and the sheets smelled clean and spicy as she snuggled into them. Heavens, that had been a horrible dream. Sneaking aboard an alien spaceship? She couldn't even imagine doing such a thing, although if it would have given her the chance to find her sister, she wouldn't have hesitated. The thought of her sister and little Charlie brought the familiar wave of sadness, and she was no longer content to snuggle into her bed. With a deep sigh, she sat up—and froze.

This wasn't her bedroom; this wasn't even one of the inexpensive hotel rooms where she spent so much time when she was on the road. Curved white metal walls surrounded the bed, forming a cozy cabin. On her right, there was a desk and what looked like an oversized recliner, but on her left... On her left was a huge window and through the window all she could see was stars.

The memories came rushing back—the park, the spaceship, Kwaret, and then Cestov.

How had she ended up here? And why was she wearing only half of the Vedeckian uniform? The oversized top reached the middle of her thighs, but she still felt uncomfortably exposed. And where was Cestov?

Climbing hastily out of the bed, she searched for her missing pants. The pristine room showed nothing out of place, but she discovered two concealed doors. Behind one she found a small closet, but her pants weren't included in the neat array of clothing. The next door revealed a spotless white bathroom, including—oh joy of joys—an actual toilet and shower. Even though she didn't know how long she would be alone, after a week of sponge baths, the shower was too tempting to resist.

A few minutes later she had managed to figure out the controls and was standing naked under a flow of hot water. Had anything ever felt better? She had a sudden flash of memory, of being cradled against a large, warm chest as Cestov had carried her to the ship. That had felt surprisingly good. In fact, she had a faint, uneasy recollection that she might have started kissing his neck. Even the distant memory caused her nipples to tighten and when she ran the cleansing cloth between her legs, the slippery heat was from more than just the water.

She couldn't remember ever feeling so instantly attracted to someone before. Even though she lived the nomadic life of a performer, she'd always had the rock-solid foundation her sister had provided to ground her carefree hippie image. Over the years she'd had a few casual relationships—usually with a fellow musician—but on the whole, she slept alone in all those empty hotel rooms. And yet here she was, her body warm with desire for an alien who she had met only hours ago. Perhaps it was just because it had been so long, perhaps she just needed to take the edge off...

She moved the cloth more slowly, teasing the rapidly hardening pearl of her clit while she tugged at her stiff nipples with her other hand. Mmm, that felt good, but she needed more. Her alien's image came to mind and she imagined him stepping up behind her, cupping her breasts with those big strong hands before sliding one down between her legs, circling her throbbing clit until she exploded.

"Cestov!" she cried as her body shuddered into a brief, hard climax.

The door flew open.

## CHAPTER EIGHT

Cestov threw open the door to the sanitary facility when Mariah cried out his name, prepared to defend her from any threat. Instead, he froze at the sight of his female, naked in the shower, her pale skin flushed pink while one hand plucked at a swollen red peak and the other dipped between softly curved thighs. Her fragrance filled the room, sending his cock into an immediate throbbing erection. He took a step towards her before he realized that she had not invited him to join her.

"Do you need assistance?"

His words seemed to shock her out of her frozen position, and she gasped, trying to cover her lush breasts with one arm and her delightful little cunt with the other.

"No! Turn around. Please."

He obediently, if reluctantly, turned away from her. "You are sure that you do not need my help? You called for me."

"I... I..."

Her voice stuttered to a stop and he suddenly realized why she had called out his name. She had been thinking of him while she pleasured herself. His cock jerked at the thought and he came close to embarrassing himself.

"Do you have a towel?" she asked, her voice shaky.

"Behind the panel to your right." He knew he should leave the room, but what if she had other questions? What if she slipped on the wet surface? And she had not asked him to leave.

He heard the panel close and risked a glance over his shoulder. She had wrapped the large white cloth around her body, but her bare shoulders rose above it, her delicate skin still flushed and glowing. The wet mass of her hair tumbled down over the tempting swell of her breasts. She looked up and met his eyes and the color on her cheeks deepened, but she gave him a tremulous smile.

"Thank you for the use of your shower."

He forced himself not to offer her the use of anything on his ship and merely nodded.

"Perhaps I could trouble you for a few more things?"

"Of course," he said eagerly.

"Do you have a comb?"

"A comb?" The word did not translate.

"You use it to untangle your hair." She took a peek up at his head and smiled again, more genuinely this time. "Well, if you have hair."

"Ah. I'm afraid... No, wait a minute. I may have something."

He hurried back into the main room, kneeling against the far wall to search through the one storage space he had set aside for personal mementos from his travels. She followed him, leaning against the wall and raking her fingers through her hair as she watched. He forced himself not to pay attention to the long bare legs beneath the towel or the knowledge that she was naked beneath it.

"I do not have many personal possessions," he explained as

he searched. "It is difficult to accumulate much when you are always—"

"—on the move?" she finished. "I know what you mean. I travel light as well."

"You are a traveler?" A delicate female? Who accompanied her? Who protected her?

"I'm a singer—that means I have to go wherever there is a gig, a job. It requires a lot of traveling but it's all I ever wanted to do." She gave him a rueful smile. "I never really minded moving around."

"I understand," he admitted. "I always enjoyed the traveling life but Bratan grew tired of it."

"Bratan?"

"My brother. He is the one for whom I search."

"I remember you said he might be on the ship Kwaret was trying to contact. Were you able to reach them?"

"Yes. As it turns out, they were already on their way. They received Kwaret's signal but apparently the return signal was not transmitting. They should have landed on Driguera only a few hours after we left."

"And your brother?"

"He was not on board." Despair washed over him. It would have made perfect sense for his brother to have joined the crew of another ship—this was the only life they had ever really known—but the captain had never heard of him. The best he could offer was to suggest that he check the records on Trevelor. Because so many refugees traveled to the planet, either to put down roots or on their way to another destination, they had an extensive database of information on the visitors.

"I'm so sorry." Mariah came and stood next to him, placing a hand on his shoulder, her delicate scent filling his head. His tail wrapped around her ankle and he took comfort from her presence. "I understand more than you think. I'm searching for my sister and my nephew."

"They were taken?"

"Yes, a year ago by the crew of the same ship that brought me here."

"They will be questioned," he assured her.

She shook her head. "We already know that they were given to another Vedeckian commander. Kwaret said that he's dead now but he was last on Trevelor."

"I will do everything I can to assist you," he promised. "We can search together."

"Thank you, Cestov." Her eyes filled with tears, then she bent forward and brushed a quick kiss to his cheek. The brief touch burned like fire and he had to force himself to return to his search rather than demanding more.

"Here." He held up the Dinglian hopper triumphantly. Five narrow prongs were suspended at the end of a long elaborately carved handle.

Mariah looked at it, then burst into laughter.

"Is something wrong?"

"I think that is intended as an eating utensil, rather than a comb."

"I'm sorry."

"Don't be. I appreciate you trying to help. And actually..." She took the hopper. "It might work."

She applied the prongs to her hair, then winced. "Oww. This might be a little harder than I thought."

"Let me assist you."

Before she could object, he placed a pillow on the floor and guided her to a seated position while he sat behind her on the bed. He would have preferred to have her on his lap, but he didn't want to frighten her. With careful fingers, he started at the ends of the long, damp strands and began to untangle her glorious hair.

After a tense moment, Mariah relaxed into Cestov's touch as he gently combed through her hair with what she suspected was actually some type of ceremonial fork. She kept expecting him to pull her hair, but his hands wielded the makeshift comb with astonishing deftness and she gradually settled back against him. She had always loved having her hair played with and it reminded her of when Judith would comb her hair when she was little. A tear rolled down her cheek.

"What is wrong? Did I hurt you?" Alarm filled his voice.

"No, not at all. I was just thinking of my sister."

He seemed to debate with himself, then he lifted her onto his lap with impressive ease. Perhaps she should have protested, but even without the ale, she found herself relaxing into his embrace.

"Were you very close?" he asked.

"Yes. And no." She smiled up at him and wiggled a little closer. "She's eight years older than I am and she practically raised me. My mother died when I was born and even though we had nannies when we were little, she's the one I remember taking care of me. But our personalities are like night and day. She always wanted a peaceful life—a home, a steady job, a child. I wanted to travel, to sing, to do something exciting with my life. We fought about that more often than I like to remember, but we loved each other very much."

Her memories consumed her, and she could feel the tears threatening again but she forced them aside and looked up at Cestov. "What about you? Is your brother older or younger than you?"

"Younger. By less than a minute." He smiled at her shock, but she could see the sadness in his eyes.

"You're twins?"

"Yes. It is very unusual for my people."

"You must have been close."

"I thought we were." His face darkened. "I thought we wanted the same kind of life, but then he began to talk about impossible things. About settling down, having a family."

"Impossible?"

"There are no females of our species. There will be no families."

"But I thought... Kwaret said something about Cires being compatible with other races?"

"What?!" After his initial shock, he shook his head. "I do not believe that to be true. He must have misunderstood. My father searched for many years to find that hope for us without success. But Bratan never stopped dreaming. The last fight we had—I told him he was a fool, told him that he could never father a child. I refused to consider his suggestion that we sell the *Wanderer* and settle down on a planet."

"What happened?"

"He left. When I woke the next morning, he was gone. He left a note saying that he had to go and find his own dream. *His* dream. It was only then that I truly understood that what I thought had been our dreams had only belonged to me. I tried to find him, to apologize, but he was gone."

He looked so sad that she reached up and kissed his cheek again. Warm and slightly textured beneath her lips, the feel of his skin tempted her to linger but she reluctantly started to pull away. As she did, he turned his head and then his mouth covered hers.

## CHAPTER NINE

Cestov kissed her, his mouth firm but gentle, and after a brief hesitation, she relaxed into his embrace. He felt so good, smelled so good, and the feel of his mouth against hers reawakened the hunger she had felt in the shower. She opened her mouth, just a little, and that small acceptance was enough. He took over, parting her lips and diving into her mouth as if he were a starving man. His taste swept over her—spicy, intoxicating. Her head spun as if she were drinking more of the Drigueran ale and she moaned, pressing herself closer. He responded just as urgently, one big hand coming down to cup her bottom and press her against the massive bar of his erection. Oh my. Her nipples peaked, her belly ached, and all she wanted was to explore more of this delicious sensation.

It took a moment for her to realize that the bells she heard were not due to his kiss.

"What's that?" she asked breathlessly, pulling away far enough that their lips parted.

"The door alarm. Ignore it," he growled, and tugged her back into his arms.

Before he could begin kissing her again, the bell chimed a second time. With a muttered curse, he deposited her carefully on the bed, and stood up. He took one step towards the door, then turned back and grabbed a blanket, throwing it over her lap. She blushed as she remembered that she was only clothed in a towel.

As he reached the door, the bell sounded a third time, and he yanked it open with a low growl.

"What the hell do you want?"

"Not me," Maldost protested. "Her."

For a minute her heart skipped a beat. Her? Did he already have a woman? She had known one too many musicians with a woman in every town. But before her doubts could really set in, the younger male thrust a small pink bundle into Cestov's arms.

"She wandered away from her mother and somehow managed to make it up the stairs into the main corridor. I'm sure she was looking for you."

"Did you leave the door to the cargo bay open?"

"No." Maldost shuffled his feet, then the furry head drooped. "At least I don't think so."

"I do not need to remind you that you are responsible for the wellbeing of the slonga," Cestov said sternly.

Slonga? Curiosity drew her to her feet and over to his side. Maldost took one look at her, flushed a deep purple, and fled with an unintelligible excuse.

"Did I do something to offend him?"

"No, but he has most likely never seen a female wearing so little clothing."

She looked down and blushed again. Oops. She had been too interested in finding out about the mysterious wanderer to worry about the blanket and was back to being clad only in a towel. While she felt surprisingly comfortable around Cestov in the scanty garb, she hadn't intended to flash the younger male. She hastily stepped back as he closed the door panel and focused on his bundle instead.

"What—who is that?"

She had never seen anything quite like it. In some ways, it resembled a small elephant—if an elephant had pink shaggy fur and six legs. As she stared, the small creature raised its head and looked at her. Its ears flared, larger even than elephant ears, but almost translucent and covered in a delicate pink and purple pattern that reminded her of exotic butterfly wings.

"Oh my, she's gorgeous. May I touch her?"

The little creature was still regarding her with big dark eyes and when she cautiously extended a finger, it shrank back into Cestov's arms.

"Do not worry, little one," he said soothingly. "Mariah is a friend. She isn't going to hurt you."

A moment later, the tiny trunk extended, cautiously wrapping around Mariah's finger and she gasped in delight. Moving slowly, she gently stroked the small trunk, covered in the softest, most delicate pink fur. A minute later, Cestov's tail wrapped around them both, enclosing the three of them in what felt like a hug. Warmth filled her and she looked up to see Cestov smiling down at her. It felt like they were enclosed in their own little bubble, like a... like a family. How much she had missed that feeling.

"Maldost said she wandered away? From where?"

"From her mother. The calves were only born a few days ago and she seems to have bonded with me."

He looked oddly bemused by the fact but from the gentle way he cradled the small creature, she wasn't at all surprised.

"Are you going to take her back?"

"Yes. Would you like to meet her mother?"

"Very much." She cast a rueful look down at herself. "But perhaps it would be best to put on some clothes first."

"What a shame," he said and arched a brow ridge.

"I'm not wandering around the ship in a towel." That reminded her... "Umm, do you know what happened to my pants?" She could feel her cheeks coloring to the same shade as the slonga's fur.

"You stripped them off when we returned here last night. Unfortunately, you ripped them in the process."

She winced. "I hope I didn't do anything too embarrassing?"

"Not at all. Although it was an interesting dance..."

"Dance?" She gave him a horrified stare. "I was dancing?"

"Well, perhaps twirling is a better word."

His lips twitched and she burst out laughing. "You're teasing me. Aren't you?"

"Only a little. You did twirl a few times, but then you almost fell over your pant legs so you stripped them off. You promised me a—what was it? Oh yes, a dance of the seven veils."

She was almost afraid to ask. "Did I do it?"

"No. You, err, stumbled onto the bed while you were trying to take off your pants. Then you informed me that it was big enough to share and fell asleep."

Oh lord. She didn't know which was worse, that she had acted so wantonly or that he seemed so amused. The heat rose in her cheeks again.

"I'm sorry."

"Do not be sorry." His tail moved from where it was still wrapped around her hand to circle her waist. "You were delightful. I have never seen someone move so freely, so gracefully."

The look in his eyes made her catch her breath and her

embarrassment faded away. She took a step towards him and then the baby slonga mewed.

"Sorry, little one," he said, stroking the small head apologetically. "We will get you back to your mother in just a minute."

"Uh, clothes?"

"There is no female clothing on board—"

And why did that make her happy?

"But I would be honored if you would wear something of mine."

With an appreciative glance at his big body, she shook her head.

"I don't think anything of yours is going to fit me. But I can try if you want," she added hastily at his distressed look.

"Here. Can you hold Lilat?"

He carefully passed her the baby slonga. The warm little body snuggled against her, unexpectedly heavy, but delightfully soft and cuddly.

"What a good girl," she cooed, and Lilat's trunk patted her cheek.

Cestov rummaged through his closet, returning a moment later with an oversized shirt and a few sashes.

"The shirt will be too large but that means it will cover most of your body. I thought perhaps you could use the sash to adjust the fit? It is only a temporary solution. We can attempt to cut something down to size later."

"We can try," she said a little doubtfully. Sewing had never been one of her strengths. "But for right now, let's see what I can do with this. You'd better take Lilat back again."

He reached for the slonga and his fingers grazed her breast. She gasped, a rush of heat sweeping over her at even that casual touch. He froze, then carefully gathered the calf back into his arms.

"I'll just go in the bathroom and change." She grabbed the clothes and departed, her cheeks burning once again.

Cestov stared at the closed door after Mariah. Having her here in his cabin seemed so right. Already, the simple space felt warmer, her delicate fragrance filling the space and making it feel like a home. Although she seemed to understand his need to keep his personal possessions few because of his travels, he was already thinking of what he could do to make the space more appropriate for her. Some pillows, perhaps? In soft colors that suited her gentle beauty? An orgat rug from Crumella? At the thought of her pale golden body stretched out across the luxuriant fibers, his shaft hardened.

*Stop that,* he told himself. *You don't need to build a home for her. You are just taking her to Trevelor. This is a temporary arrangement, nothing more.* The knowledge didn't help.

Lilat mewed and he raised her up to his face, his tail curled protectively around her back.

"Are you hungry, little one? You shouldn't wander away like that."

Her trunk reached out and patted his face and his heart ached as he remembered that she too would be leaving him. He had become attached to the small creature.

"How does this look?"

Mariah appeared in the doorway and his mouth went dry. He had given her his smallest shirt, but it still swamped her diminutive frame. The neckline slipped off one shoulder to reveal her delicate collarbone, while the hem reached only to her knees, displaying a tempting expanse of pale flesh. She had tied the sash around her waist in a complicated knot, highlighting her lush curves.

"You look beautiful," he told her sincerely.

Her cheeks turned that delightful shade of pink again. A most engaging phenomenon.

"Do you have my sandals?"

He fought to hide his grin. She had kicked them off as soon as he put her down in the cabin the previous night. One of them had hit him in the head but he had been too entranced by her actions to object. She moved so gracefully, as if she were dancing to music only she could hear. After she fell asleep, he found the other shoe where it had landed on top of his desk.

"They are in the storage unit."

She flashed him a quick smile as she retrieved the sandals, then bent down to put them on. The fabric tightened across the luscious curves of her ass and his cock jerked again. Had he ever been this responsive to a female before? Over the years, he had tried a few times to have a relationship with a female, even though he had known he could only find true fulfillment with a Cire woman. None of those females had ever seemed right and his cock had been slow to respond. No one had ever aroused him the way that she did simply with her scent and her movements.

Mariah came to join him and reached over to stroke Lilat's soft fur.

"She's so sweet. How did you end up with her?"

"I'm a trader. On our last trip to Srashiman, Maldost was supposed to be trading for pristidian seedlings. He ended up with her mother instead," he said grimly.

"He bought a pregnant female?"

"In his defense, he did not know she was pregnant. And by the time I realized what he had done, we were already several days away. I was so focused on trying to come up with another lead on my brother's whereabouts that I didn't want to take the time to return."

"You have to take her back."

Fuck. He knew she was right—he had been coming to the same conclusion over the past few days. Despite the financial loss and the not inconsiderable risk of running into the Patrol, it was the right thing to do.

Mariah's eyes filled with tears. "You took her away from her planet. She's all alone in a strange new place."

He suspected that her tears were for far more than the slonga, but his tail circled her waist and pulled her close.

"I will make sure that the slonga—and you—get home." It was a vow.

## CHAPTER TEN

Mariah wiped her eyes and smiled up at Cestov. He sounded so sincere and she believed him, but she had been thinking more of her sister's situation than hers. As much as she longed to find Judith and Charlie, she was enjoying this adventure more than she had expected. Especially now that she was off that dreadful Vedeckian ship and with Cestov. The thought of the Vedeckian ship made her remember Kwaret.

"You said that the Cire ship was going to stop the Vedeckians, right? Have you heard anything else?"

"No, but I'll check as soon as we return this little one to her mother," he promised.

He led her down the corridor to a wide door panel, opening it to reveal a catwalk and a set of stairs that descended into a cargo hold uncomfortably similar to that of the Vedeckian ship.

*It's just cargo*, she reminded herself. *He's nothing like them.*

One side of the space had the all too familiar arrangement of storage containers strapped into a complicated structure. A waist-high fence enclosed the other side, surrounding an area filled with sweet-smelling grasses. The mother slonga was stretched out in the bedding, chewing lazily, but she stood up and bellowed when they approached. She was smaller than Mariah had expected, no bigger than a small pony, but her ears flared out into fluttering curtains of shimmering color.

"Now, now, Tajka. This is Mariah. She's a friend."

"She's so beautiful," Mariah whispered. "Those ears are amazing."

"And valuable," Maldost said as he appeared from one end of the room with an armload of bedding. "They are being taken because of that. That's why it's illegal to remove them from the Srashiman system."

"Oh, no. That's terrible."

Maldost ducked his head and looked at Cestov from under his eyelashes. "That's one of the reasons I took her in a trade. I was afraid of what would happen to her if someone else bought her."

Cestov sighed. "Is there anything else about this transaction that you're not telling me?"

"No. I think that's it." Maldost's ears perked up and he grinned.

He reminded her so much of one of the young musicians she had played with in New Orleans. She had been there for a month-long festival and had gotten to know the young man quite well. He was a brilliant musician, barely out of high school, but he had the same thoughtless enthusiasm and big, awkward body—although his hadn't been covered with fur. She had missed him when she moved on.

One of the downsides of the traveling life was how quickly you lost track of people and the connections you made. All you could hope to do was to run into them further down the road. At least she'd had Judith to provide her with a sense of permanence. This past year without her sister had made her only too aware of how lonely life on the road could be when there was no home to visit in between. All of her protests about not wanting to be tied down had sounded shallow when she had no roots at all.

Fighting down the surge of loneliness, she moved a little closer to Cestov and breathed in his spicy scent. Something about him comforted her, made her feel less alone.

He reached over the low fence and deposited Lilat at her mother's feet. The slonga's trunk reached out to tuck the calf close to her as she resumed her previous position. Cestov's tail wrapped around Mariah's waist in a way that also felt protective, although not in the least bit maternal, and she leaned against him as she watched the other calves scamper closer as they realized it was mealtime. Their coats were in various shades of pink, ranging from a very pale pearly hue to a deep, almost lavender shade.

"They really are adorable," she said.

"And remarkably adaptable. They seem to be doing just fine on the ship," Maldost said eagerly.

"They can't stay here. You know that," Cestov said firmly and Maldost's ears drooped. Cestov turned back to her. "I suspect they're all going to take a nap as soon as they finish eating. Would you like to see the rest of the ship?"

"Yes, very much. I've never—" She stopped abruptly and gave him a rueful smile. "I was going to say I'd never been aboard a spaceship before but of course, I was on board the Vedeckian ship."

His brow ridges drew together. "We should go check and see if the Cire ship has been successful in arresting them."

"Yes, and I'd like to know what happened with Kwaret."

"Very well." He turned towards the stairs and Maldost started to follow them. "Maldost, you need to clean up after the little ones."

"What? Again?" The big shoulders slumped. "Yes, boss."

"I guess he's in charge of cleaning up the poop?" she asked once they were back in the corridor.

"Yes. The responsibility is good for him. It's somewhat of a punishment for purchasing her in the first place, although I'm sure he was motivated by compassion. He has an unfortunate tendency to pick up any stray animal that he finds, and this is not the life for them. Although..." he looked back at the hold regretfully, "I wish sometimes that it could be."

"Why did Maldost decide to be a trader?"

"His homeworld was devastated by the Red Death. You are familiar with the plague?"

"Yes, Kwaret told me about it, although I have a hard time imagining that amount of devastation."

Shadows crossed his face. "It was a terrible time. Many of the planets took drastic measures in an attempt to eliminate it—Maldost's world was one of them. They burnt much of their land in an attempt to isolate the danger but all it did was destroy most of the natural environment. There was little left for him there."

Her heart ached for the young male. "I'm so sorry. No wonder he's so sympathetic to strays."

"A little too sympathetic, I am afraid. And now I suspect he has bonded with the slonga."

"And you haven't?"

His lips twitched. "Perhaps."

"I know it will be hard for you to return her."

"Yes. It's always hard to let something go once you have made a connection."

From the way he looked at her as he spoke, she suspected he meant more than just the slonga and a lump formed in her throat. She already imagined she would feel the same way about leaving him behind. *Judith and Charlie*, she reminded herself. *You have to find them and get them home.*

Once they were on the bridge, he introduced her to Plovac, the navigator. The tall, thin male had pale blue skin, with spiked ridges down his arms and a long hollow face with deeply sunken solid black eyes. Despite his rather creepy appearance, his smile was friendly.

"Welcome aboard, Human Mistress."

"Uh, thanks. Please call me Mariah."

"Yes, Mistress Mariah," he said solemnly, and she hid her smile.

"Have you heard back from the *Defiance*?" Cestov asked.

"Yes. The ship was taken into custody. Two of the human females and their children are already on their way back to Earth."

"What about the third woman?" she asked anxiously. "Kwaret said they were going to try and sell her at some kind of auction."

Plovac made an odd wheezing noise that she eventually decided was laughter.

"It appears that they had some difficulty with that plan. She was not grateful to be recovered by the Cire. After some discussion, it appears that she will be going to Trevelor as well."

"Going to Trevelor? Why?"

"She is looking for her daughter. They think she was taken during the previous abductions."

They had taken her child? She couldn't imagine anything worse. One of the few things she had consoled herself with over the past year was the hope that Judith and Charlie were together, even though she was now alone. How much worse it must have been to know your child was out there alone.

"I thought the *Defiance* intercepted that abduction. Why was the child not returned?" Cestov asked, his brows furrowing.

"I don't know. Perhaps they did not know where to take her?"

"From what Kwaret said, Trevelor seems like a peaceful place," she said. "I hope they found a good home for the baby."

And possibly for Judith and Charlie. Kwaret seemed doubtful that they had ended up on the planet, but he didn't really know. Wouldn't that be a wonderful surprise if she found them so quickly?

"If there is a Cire colony on Trevelor, the baby would have been more than welcome," Cestov assured her. "But I think most races now know to value all children."

After spending a few more minutes with Plovac, Cestov showed her around the rest of the ship. The main level held the bridge, along with the crew quarters and living areas, plus additional storage. The engine room was at the far end, above the actual engines. He introduced her to Servisa, the mechanic, a short, stocky male with dark red skin and two sets of horns. He reminded her a little too much of her childhood image of the devil but like Plovac, he was extremely polite.

Cestov showed her a large workout room, then pointed out a small medical lab with a grim look on his face.

"Do you have a doctor on board?" she asked curiously.

"Of a kind. I found him on one of the inner planets, being attacked by a group of ruffians. I stopped the fight and dragged him back to the *Wanderer*."

Looking at that massive body, she could easily imagine him putting a rapid end to any kind of fight and the thought sent an unexpected thrill through her. She forced her mind back to his words.

"Apparently, Maldost isn't the only one who takes in strays," she said dryly.

He shook his head. "Not always with the best judgment, I'm afraid. He is more interested in drinking than healing."

"I've worked with more than a few musicians like that. Some of them manage to handle it. With others, it just takes over their lives and they end up losing their careers."

"You said you were a singer. Will you sing for me?"

A completely unexpected shyness swept over her. She couldn't even remember the last time she had been intimidated by a request to sing, but somehow this was different.

"Maybe later," she said, trying not to blush.

After the tour, he took her back to his cabin and they tried, not very successfully, to make her another outfit. In the end, he took a bedsheet and they cut it into two rectangles. He fastened the sides and shoulders together using some type of seaming device and she dropped it over her head. With the sash pulling in the waist, it actually wasn't too bad. It reminded her of something an ancient Greek maiden would wear. The thin material felt soft and comfortable against her skin—although she discovered some unexpected consequences when she went to show it to him.

"What do you think?"

The obvious hunger in his eyes made her own body respond. The clothing attempt had put them in constant close proximity, especially during some awkward attempts to measure her, and she hadn't been able to avoid noticing that he seemed to maintain an almost continuous erection. Her nipples stiffened and his eyes dropped to her breasts. When she looked down, the stiff peaks were clearly visible through the thin fabric. Oops.

"I think this will work," she said quickly. "Now what should we do?"

The hunger in his eyes increased and she realized what she had said.

He stalked towards her—there was no other way to put it— and she waited breathlessly, her knees trembling just a little.

"I have a suggestion," he purred as he reached her. His tail wrapped around her waist and pulled her snuggly against that big body. She could feel the rigid line of his erection—his very large erection—against her stomach.

"I..."

Even though speaking her mind had never been a problem before, this time she found herself speechless. A very large part of her just wanted to give in to her impulses and test out the promise in those dark eyes, but she could almost hear her sister's cautionary voice in her head. He was an alien and she really didn't know him, no matter how much she felt as if she did. No matter how safe he made her feel with the heat of his body surrounding her and his spicy scent filling her senses...

"Do not be afraid, Mariah," he assured her, taking in her confusion. His voice softened. "I would never urge you to do anything you do not wish to do."

"I know that." She truly believed it. "It's just that..."

"Yes?"

"I can't stay!" she burst out. "I have to find my sister and her little boy. I have to take them home so we can be a family again."

He didn't move away, but she felt him stiffen. When she looked up at him, he didn't look angry, he looked devastated.

"What is it?" she asked softly.

"That's what my brother wanted," he said quietly. "A family. I told him that we were already a family, but he wanted more. He wanted a mate, a child. No matter how impossible his dream."

"I'm so sorry." She leaned into him and put her arms around him. His tail tightened around her waist at the same time that his arms enclosed her. Despite his still obvious erection, this felt more like comfort than desire and she nestled against him, unexpectedly content.

## CHAPTER ELEVEN

Cestov finally stepped back and she fought the urge to cling to him. It was for the best, she reminded herself, even though her body ached with frustrated desire.

"Since you have so callously refused my advances," he said solemnly, "perhaps we should go and visit the slonga before my little Lilat escapes again."

"I wasn't being callous," she started to protest, then saw the smile in those big dark eyes and shook her head. "Never mind. Yes, I would love to see them again."

He led her to the door and his tail curled around her wrist. She rubbed it gently, exploring the small nubs that covered the surface, and heard him catch his breath.

"I'm sorry. Is it sensitive?"

"Very much so. When you caress it like that, it is almost as if you are stroking my cock."

The image made her clit throb, but she resolutely ignored it, even as she started to pull her hand away. He immediately placed his hand over hers.

"Please do not stop touching me. I've never felt such pleasure before."

"No other woman has ever stroked your tail?" she tried to joke, attempting a smile despite a sudden pang of jealousy.

"No," he said seriously. "My tail has never shown an interest in a female before."

"Really?" She couldn't help feeling oddly flattered, especially considering that his tail had pretty much been touching her continuously since the moment they met. "Is that unusual?"

"If you were a Cire female, then I would take it as a sign that we were destined mates." Her heart skipped a beat before he continued. "But unfortunately, that is no longer possible since all of our females died during the Red Death."

"And there's no chance of you finding a destined mate with a female of another race?" *Why was she even pursuing this?*

"No. My father was quite clear. And without a destined mate, we also cannot father children."

"You mean your, umm, equipment doesn't work?" she asked, shooting a discreet glance at the seemingly ever-present bulge of his cock. She certainly hadn't seen any signs that it was deficient in any way.

"No." He laughed. "I assure you that my cock is quite functional, but my seed is not fertile. I have never even knotted inside a female."

"Knotted?"

"The base of my shaft swells, to lock me inside my mate while my seed takes root."

Oh my. The thought aroused her a lot more than she thought it should and she could feel the damp heat between her legs. His thin nostrils flared.

"You are aroused."

"Yes," she admitted. "But it doesn't change anything."

"Of course not, my miri."

"What did you call me?"

"My miri. It is a rare yellow flower that grows on Osvet, blooming only once every five years. Our ship landed there during the bloom period and I have never forgotten. The flower had long yellow petals with pink streaks." He stroked a finger down her hair. "And the sweetest fragrance I have ever encountered. Until now, that is."

She knew her cheeks were bright red again, but she leaned into him. "That's the nicest thing anyone has ever said to me."

"I speak only the truth."

He stopped and she realized that he was about to kiss her again. Her good sense had abandoned her—she wanted his kiss. But as his head lowered, Maldost appeared in the open doorway.

"Boss! Am I glad to see you!"

Cestov sighed and raised his head. "What is it, Maldost?"

"Your little Lilat is leading a revolution." Maldost sounded exceptionally frazzled. "All of the calves are out of the pen now."

"All right. Let's see if we can calm them down."

Together, the three of them tried to corral the four little slonga, who seemed to be having the time of their lives as they squealed with glee and darted through the maze of containers. The mother watched with surprising calm.

Cestov captured Lilat first because she ran to him as soon as she saw him. He handed her to Mariah.

"Perhaps you could hold her and stay with Tajka while I help Maldost?" He looked at the pen, then shook his head. "Never mind. You don't want to go in there."

"I don't mind, as long as it's fairly clean."

"But your dress..."

"You'll just have to help me make another one." She couldn't resist. "Unless you want me to run around naked."

Ignoring the flare of heat in his eyes, she turned and sashayed over to the pen, conscious of his eyes on her the whole time. She climbed over the fence and went to sit in the sweet-smelling bedding next to Tajka with Lilat in her lap.

"He's certainly good for a girl's ego," she whispered to the slonga. A moment later, Tajka's trunk curled around her shoulders and she laughed. "And so are you."

They all watched as Cestov and Maldost chased the other calves. When Cestov finally caught one, he brought it over to her as well. The little male was by no means as calm as his sister and squirmed restlessly.

"What's his name?"

"Tomat."

"Hush now, Tomat," she whispered.

Without consciously thinking about it, she began singing a soft lullaby. It seemed to work, and he settled down in her lap as well.

"This is Hari." Maldost handed her another calf.

Her singing worked on him as well and it wasn't long before Cestov handed her the third male and collapsed next to her.

"And finally, Dickan."

She added him to the pile, continuing to sing until all four of the infants dozed peacefully. When she brought the song to a close, she looked up to see both Maldost and Cestov staring at her.

"What? Did I do something wrong?"

"You have a beautiful voice, my miri," Cestov said, his eyes warm and appreciative.

"Thank you." The compliment felt more significant than any review she had ever received, and she fought to hide her pleasure, focusing on the sleeping calves instead. "Should we get out of here before they wake up?"

She tucked Lilat against her mother's side and Cestov lifted her easily to her feet. Tajka's trunk patted her arm, then she used it to rearrange the calves to her satisfaction before lowering her own head.

"Thank you," Maldost said. "I didn't think they were ever going to calm down."

"I'm guessing they needed some exercise." She looked around the big cargo bay. "Is there anything in here that they can hurt? Or that can hurt them?"

"No, I suppose not," Cestov admitted.

"Then why not let them run around?"

"What if they shit all over the place?" Maldost protested.

"Then you will just have to clean it up," Cestov said cheerfully as he swept Mariah up the stairs.

He took her to the galley and introduced her to the wonders of spaceship cooking, which seemed to consist mainly of pushing buttons.

"I could get used to this. I was never much of a cook," she admitted as they sat down to eat. "Judith tried to teach me, but I was always too impatient. I had a habit of jumping ahead without paying attention to what needed to be done next."

"You said your sister is older than you?"

"Yes, by eight years. She helped raise me." Her throat closed. "She was so good to me, more like a mother than a sister most of the time. I wish she hadn't waited so long to have Charlie. She was in her forties when she finally decided that I wasn't going to grow up and went after her own dream."

"You seem fully grown to me," he said appreciatively.

"In years, yes. I'm practically over the hill."

"I do not understand. What hill?"

"It's just an expression. It means my youth is behind me."

"But your sister did not think so?"

"She wanted me to stop traveling. To get a job singing somewhere close to her."

"But you did not want this?"

"No. I always thought I was one gig away from my big break. One job away from the opportunity that would change everything," she clarified. "And then I would be a star."

"I think I understand. We always used to joke about finding that one cargo that would make our fortune." He looked away from her, his eyes distant. "At least I was joking. I was content with my life. I now know my brother was not."

"And I was pretty happy with mine. Well, most of the time." Those empty hotel rooms flashed through her mind. "But I think part of it was because I knew I could always come back to her. That I had a home and a family waiting for me while I explored."

"Bratan was my family. I cannot forgive myself for not realizing that he needed more."

She reached over and laid her hand on his. After a long silence, he sighed and changed the subject.

They spent most of the afternoon talking, not about anything important, but he told her some of his adventures as a trader and she told him about her life on the road. They both very carefully avoided talking about their loved ones and the hope that they would find them on Trevelor.

When the evening meal rolled around, they made it together—or at least she helped him push the buttons—and then the rest of the crew joined them. The doctor appeared for the first time. Like Plovac, he was tall and thin, but he had milky white skin and waist-length red hair tied back in an elaborate series of braids. Two small antennae rose up from each temple. As with the rest of the crew, he was polite, but he ate very little and spoke even less.

After the meal, Maldost bashfully asked her to sing for them.

"Are you sure? I doubt you would know any of the songs that I know," she said doubtfully.

He shrugged. "I did not know the song you sang to the slongas, but I enjoyed it."

She cast a helpless glance at Cestov, but he only smiled and urged her on. After a quick survey of her repertoire, she started with Jimmy Buffet's "Son of a Sailor." She suspected that they would appreciate the sailor analogy and by the second chorus, they were humming along.

When she finished, all of them snapped their fingers in what seemed to be a round of applause and she laughed. Why had she been so hesitant?

The rest of the evening passed with her entertaining a very appreciative audience. Even Whovian stayed in the lounge, although she noticed his fingers shaking when he applauded her. For the last song, she sang "What a Wonderful World," letting the words trickle down into silence. No round of applause this time, just an appreciative silence that meant more than applause ever would.

"That's all, gentlemen."

"Thank you, Mistress Mariah," Plovac said gravely. "A most enjoyable evening."

"You're welcome."

Each of the others thanked her and wandered off, leaving her alone with Cestov. He hadn't said much throughout the evening, although she was always conscious of his eyes watching her and his tail frequently grazed her wrist or ankle.

"Was that all right? I didn't mean to take up the whole evening."

"You are very talented, my miri," he said softly. "I understand why you wish to share that gift with the world."

"I love to sing," she agreed, "but I also spent a lot of time waiting for fame and fortune to come my way."

"To be a, what did you call it? A star?"

"Exactly. Now I'm not so sure if that's what I really wanted." She grinned up at him. "Maybe five aliens on a spaceship was my ideal audience all along."

"I hope so." He paused as if he was about to say something else, then shook his head. "Let's go check on Tajka and the calves."

"Are you sure Lilat is the one who chases you?" she teased as she followed him down the stairs. "It seems like you miss her just as much."

"It is a different experience, I must admit. She is so small and helpless, but she trusts me."

"She knows you'd never hurt her," she said softly as they reached the pen.

The fence had been removed but all of the calves were curled up against Tajka's stomach, her trunk blanketing them. She looked up at them with her big, dark eyes as they approached and lifted her trunk briefly to touch each of them.

"Good night, Tajka," Mariah whispered.

At the top of the stairs, Cestov started towards his cabin, then hesitated.

"It had not occurred to me until now. This ship is not equipped for passengers. There are no additional cabins."

"Do you want me to sleep with the slonga?" she teased.

"Of course not."

He looked so shocked that she relented and lightly patted the tail that was once again around her waist. "I know you wouldn't do that."

He looked at her hand on his tail and his eyes closed. She saw his fist clench and remembered what he had said earlier and snatched her hand away.

"I'm sorry."

"Please do not be sorry. It is most... enjoyable. But perhaps a little frustrating." Before she could respond, he continued, "If you will permit me to get a clean uniform, I will leave you to sleep."

"But where are you going to sleep?"

"In the lounge. There is a bed in the medical lab, but..." He made a face. "I would prefer to avoid it."

He followed her silently into the cabin, heading straight for the closet. She looked over at the bed—it was very large. Would she be crazy to suggest that he share it? No, she decided. She had absolutely no concern that he would take advantage of her. If anything, it might be the other way around, she thought ruefully, as he bent over to pick up something and she admired the way his uniform tightened around his butt.

"You can stay," she blurted out. "If you want to, I mean."

"Are you sure?" he said, spinning around so quickly that she instinctively took a step back.

'Yes. But I'm just offering to let you sleep here. Not anything else."

"Of course not." He looked at the recliner. "I could sleep there if that would make you feel more comfortable."

"No, that's all right. We can share the bed without attacking each other, right?" *She hoped.*

"I would never attack you." His eyes darkened. "I assure you that I have completely different wishes."

"That's the part I'm worried about," she muttered.

"My miri, if you are worried about this, I promise you I will be quite comfortable in the lounge."

"No, you won't." She took a deep breath. "Can you lend me a shirt again? To sleep in."

"Of course. You are welcome to anything I have."

The sincerity in his voice tugged at her. She grabbed the

shirt and escaped into the bathroom, then leaned against the door with her eyes closed. How was she supposed to resist him when he said things like that? When he looked at her as if she were the most miraculous thing he'd ever seen?

Her head and her heart were at war. She wanted to be with him, even though she knew that there was no future between them. She was not at all sure that she would be able to walk away from him with no regrets when the time came, but she suspected she might regret missing this chance just as much. Was it foolish of her? By the time she had brushed her teeth and changed into his shirt, she had reached a decision.

## CHAPTER TWELVE

"I've been thinking," Mariah said when she emerged from the sanitary facility.

"Yes?" he said absently, distracted by the sight of her once more attired in his clothing. He found it incredibly satisfying to see her wrapped in his shirt, as if his shirt were a substitute for his arms. Lucky shirt, to be touching all of that soft, tempting flesh. His cock pressed against his pants and his tail flicked back and forth impatiently when he forced himself not to step towards her and gather her in his arms. His body did not appreciate his restraint.

"Do you remember what I said earlier—about not staying?" she asked.

"Yes, I remember." The thought made his chest ache, but he understood. "I honor your commitment to your family."

"Umm, yes. But I was also thinking..."

"Yes?"

"I want to be with you," she blurted out. "While I am here."

He took one step towards her, then paused. Could he do such a thing? He already dreaded the time when they would part. How much worse would it be if she shared her body with him? He thought about his father, and how his father had faded after his mother's death. But he had always known that his father would have chosen to have that time with her over living a longer life without her. In the end, it was not a difficult decision.

"I want to be with you too."

She gave him a tentative smile, looking adorably nervous. He walked over and enclosed her in the safety of his arms and tail.

"There is no hurry, my miri. We can proceed or not—it is for you to decide."

She sighed and relaxed against him. "I know I'm being silly, but it's been a long time."

"For me as well. And no other female has ever felt or smelled so right."

"Smelled?" She tilted her head back to look up at him, her nose wrinkling.

"Your scent appeals to me like no other." He bent down and buried his face in her neck, breathing in the delicious perfume of her skin. Would she taste as wonderful? He took a slow lick and groaned. Oh, yes. Delicious. She shivered in his arms.

"Does that offend you?"

"Offend me? No," she gasped, and he realized that the tantalizing fragrance of her arousal had increased. Beneath the thin covering of his shirt, her nipples resembled hard little gems.

"Then I shall continue."

He pressed his mouth against her neck, experimenting first with his tongue, then with small kisses, and finally a careful scrape of his teeth, until he found all of the places that made her sigh and melt against him. The scent of her arousal grew stronger still, and she began shifting restlessly against him, rubbing the tight points of her nipples against his chest. His tail slipped under her shirt to stroke the soft curves of her buttocks and probe gently into the warmth between her legs. She gave a startled gasp but did not object.

Lifting her into his arms, he started to carry her to the bed but decided that perhaps his chair would be a better alternative. He did not want her to think that he expected her to give herself to him. As soon as he sat down with her in his arms, she turned towards him.

"My turn," she whispered, and before he could respond, her soft lips pressed against his neck. His cock throbbed so intensely he was afraid that he would burst from his pants at the feel of that soft little mouth against his skin. His skin was thicker than hers, of course, but he could feel the warm wetness of her mouth and could only begin to imagine what her luscious cunt would feel like. He covered one breast with his hand, delighting in the tight peak stabbing his palm, and she moaned and pushed into it. He teased the tempting bud of her nipple, then slid his hand between her thighs.

She parted them so that he could feel for himself the liquid heat of her desire. Gently running his finger between her folds, he found a swollen little button. As soon as he touched it, she cried out and clutched his arms. Ah, a pleasure receptacle. He explored, first circling the small nub, then brushing his finger across the top in slow strokes.

"Oh, yes," she whispered as he repeated the movement.

Her hand tightened on his arm, her whole body tensed, and then she shook with the intensity of her climax before sagging into his arms.

WHEN MARIAH FINALLY FOUND THE STRENGTH TO OPEN

her eyes, she expected to find Cestov smiling back at her. Instead, his face was drawn in rigid lines, his eyes blazing. He looked almost as if he were in pain.

"Cestov, is something wrong?" She realized too late that she had been clutching his tail when he brought her to orgasm. "Did I hurt you?"

"No, my miri," he said, but she could hear the strain in his voice. "I am attempting to restrain myself."

"Restrain yourself? Oh." She suddenly noticed just how hard his erection felt beneath her—an erection she had been grinding against as she came. As she started to move away, he grabbed her waist, pulling her back against him.

"Do not leave me. Please."

"I'm not going to leave you," she said quickly. "But perhaps we can make you more comfortable?"

She fumbled at his pants before giving a frustrated sigh when she realized she had no idea how to open them. "Can you open—"

Before she could finish speaking, he had freed his erection. The heavy length sprang up between them and her mouth went dry. Long, thick, and covered with the same small nubs as the rest of his skin. She ran a cautious finger down his length, wondering just how that would feel inside her, and he groaned. His tail curved up to circle a nipple, pulling on it with a gentle tug. A moment ago, she had felt completely drained. Now her excitement rose to match his. His spicy scent filled the air and she wondered almost dizzily if he tasted the same way. Precum had beaded on the tip and she ran a finger through the glistening fluid and brought it to her lips.

"Mmm, you taste delicious."

"I am sure you do as well, my miri. May I taste you?"

That sounded amazing but...

"Later," she promised and bent down to lick the tempting drop.

His hips jerked upwards so quickly that the entire head pushed into her mouth. She thought she heard a muffled apology, but she was too busy exploring his cock to pay attention. The wide head stretched her lips apart, but she still wanted more. She tried to take him deeper as she put her hand around him, or rather tried to put her hand around him since her fingers would not close around the thick length. She stroked upwards as she brought her mouth down and felt his fingers in her hair.

"If you keep doing that, I will not be able to control myself," she heard him say, but she was too busy concentrating on the thick length, relishing his exotic taste and the way his body shuddered at her touch.

She tried to take more of him, opening her mouth and tightening her grip on his shaft, increasing her rhythm until she heard him call out her name as he exploded in long pulses of liquid heat that she swallowed eagerly. When he finally slowed, she raised her head to smile at him, expecting him to be more relaxed. Instead, his face showed even more strain and she realized that the broad shaft in her hand hadn't softened.

"I need to be inside you," he said through gritted teeth.

She leaned into him, no thought of denial in her mind. "Yes."

Cestov swept Mariah up into his arms, carrying her to his bed and stripping his shirt from her impatiently. Despite the need tearing at his insides, he paused for a moment just to admire the sight of her in his bed. Her long hair spread out around her like a silken cloak, accenting the pale perfection of her body—her heavy breasts with the taut pink nipples, the gentle swell of her stomach and hips, the soft little curls between her legs veiling the tempting folds of her cunt.

She lifted her arms to him, and he gladly went to her, suppressing his need so that he could kiss her and explore more of her luscious little mouth. He could taste himself combined with her sweetness and it made him throb with need. His cock ached but he would not rush her.

"Are you sure?"

"Yes," she said, then a startled look crossed her face, and she hesitated. "You don't have a condom, do you?"

"A condom?" The word did not translate.

"To cover your, uh, shaft. To prevent pregnancy."

"I'm sorry, my miri. I cannot get you pregnant." The thought of her, ripe and swelling with his child made his cock jerk. How he wished he could have a child with her.

"My seed is not fertile until I form a mating bond with a Cire female," he explained. Something that would never happen, and yet, he had no regrets. He would choose his Mariah over any Cire female.

She bit her lip. "And disease? Is that an issue?"

"No. Whovian may not be an ideal medic but he performs regular examinations on all of the crew."

"I'm sorry for asking."

"Not at all. You are wise to look after your health. Are there any more questions?" he asked patiently, despite the need raging through his body.

She smiled up at him like the sun rising over the arc of a planet. "No, Cestov. No more questions."

He would have liked to think that he didn't fall upon her like a ravening beast, but he suspected that he would be lying to himself. He devoured her mouth and worshipped her breasts before making his way to his ultimate destination. Parting her legs, he inspected the delicate folds, flushed deep pink and glistening with her arousal. He found the small button at the top of her slit that caused her such pleasure and carefully stroked his finger across it. Her back arched, bringing her closer, and he dropped his head to taste the tempting morsel. By Granthar, he had never known such a pleasure. He licked again, eager to taste every drop of her essence, while his tail came up to explore, first sliding between her lips, then probing at her small entrance. When his tail slipped inside, he groaned at the slick, tight heat. She was so small—could she even take him?

Determined to bring her to pleasure once more, he matched the stroke of his tongue across her button with slowly increasing penetration into her tight little cunt. Her fingers clutched his shoulders as she urged him on with soft cries. He went deeper, finding a place that made her quiver, and concentrated on her pleasure button, sucking the entire nub into his mouth until he felt her body tighten around him and she climaxed in a wave of liquid heat.

Mmm, perfect. He licked up the result of her pleasure and regretfully removed his tail. He tested her with a finger, then two. Still tantalizingly tight, but her body stretched to accommodate him. He could wait no longer.

Rising over her, he notched the head of his cock at the small entrance, the dark green of his shaft shocking against her deep pink flesh. He pushed gently but her body resisted. His tail found her pleasure button and tugged. Her hips jerked upwards and he slid inside. Never had he felt anything so hot and tight, so welcoming. Her fragrance surrounded him, making his head spin with excitement and he pushed deeper, determined to bury himself in her.

"Oh." Her fingers clutched his shoulders and he dragged his gaze away from the sight of her stretched around his cock. Her eyes were wide and startled, her small blunt teeth closed on her plump lower lip.

"Is something wrong?"

"No," she said quickly. "Just so full."

"Should I withdraw?" He started to pull back, but her legs came up to circle his hips, restraining him.

"No. Just give me a minute."

It took all of his self-control to obey. His cock throbbed and his body wanted to plunge deeper, harder into the silken fist of her cunt. An idea came to him and his tail swept across her pleasure button again. Ah. He felt the rush of liquid, saw her eyes grow heavy with pleasure. He repeated the movement and her hips rose, taking him deeper.

He could wait no longer—he buried himself to the root and she took all of him, her legs still clinging to him. Tightening his grasp on her hips, he began thrusting, helpless to the instinct to take, to pleasure, to fill her with his seed. Her body shuddered and she cried out as he felt her channel convulsing around him, squeezing him impossibly tighter as he moved faster, harder. He felt his cock swell and for the first time in his life, the knot formed at the base, locking him in place as he finally, finally expelled his seed in long hot pulses, collapsing down over her as he shuddered through the exquisite pleasure.

When his knot had formed, he had heard her cry out again, had felt her tremble with her own liquid response. Now he forced himself to raise his head, to check and make sure that she was not in discomfort.

"Are you well, Mariah?"

"Well?" she raised heavy eyelids. "You can say that again."

"Why would I—"

"I mean yes, very much so." She squirmed a little and they both groaned. "I thought I was full before but... wow."

"You are not uncomfortable? I understand that it will take some time before it diminishes."

"No, I'm not uncomfortable." She wiggled again, her eyes

fluttering shut. "You know, this is actually kind of nice. You have to stay and cuddle instead of jumping up and leaving."

Shocked, he could only stare at her. "Leaving? Why would I do such a thing?"

"Some Earth males like to leave after sex," she said with a shrug that sent another ripple of pleasure through their joined bodies.

"They are fools. I can think of no greater pleasure than holding you in my arms like this."

"You're very sweet, Cestov." She raised her hand and stroked his face, small fingers soft and comforting. "I want to find my sister, and I know you want to find your brother just as much, but I'm glad that we have this time together."

"As am I, my miri. As am I."

His knot eventually went down and he reluctantly slipped free. He insisted on fetching a cleansing cloth, carefully inspecting her for damage. Her delicate folds were dark pink and slightly swollen, but she showed no discomfort when he cleansed her, and her small channel had closed back down, only a small pearl of fluid remaining at the entrance.

"You are comfortable?"

"Yes. And sleepy." She gave him a contented smile. "Are you going to sleep with me?"

"Of course." How could she even ask? "Unless you would rather I did not?"

"Don't be silly. Of course I want you to stay."

"Is that another thing that Earth males do? Not remain to sleep with the female?"

"Sometimes."

"Then they are doubly fools."

He climbed in next to her, tucking her against his body as he ordered the lights to dim. Never had he felt this level of happiness. His female warm and safe in his arms, her scent surrounding him, his seed filling her. Once again, he was struck by a vision of her ripe with child and a sharp spike of pain went to his heart that it would never be. Was this what his brother had felt? This longing for a mate and a child? How could he have been so blind as to not realize what a gift it would be?

 Mariah's breathing slowed and deepened as she slipped into sleep and he had to force himself not to clutch her against him in the vain hope that he could keep her. He had promised to help her find her sister and to see her home. He would keep that vow, no matter how much it would cost him.

## CHAPTER THIRTEEN

"Trevelor up ahead," Plovac announced.

Mariah leaned closer from her position on Cestov's lap, excited to see a new planet for the first time. She had been concealed when approaching Driguera and then asleep when they had left. She watched in amazement as the planet grew larger in the viewscreen. The landmasses and oceans looked normal enough, although the colors were deeper and richer than the ones most commonly seen in images of Earth from space.

"Not long now," Cestov said, his arms tightening around her middle.

"No," she agreed, and put her hands over his. She didn't want to leave him, didn't even want to leave this ship really. The past week had been wonderful, and she felt at home here in so many ways. The crew gathered each evening to listen to her sing and she felt comfortable with all of them, even the obviously troubled Whovian. But more than anything else, there was Cestov. She spent almost every moment with him whether they were playing with Lilat and her brothers or preparing meals or swapping tales of life on the road. Not to mention the considerable amount of time they spent in his big bed, wrapped around each other.

*You have a mission*, she reminded herself. She had to find her sister and nephew and get them back to Earth. Assuming they wanted to go, that is. What if they had found somewhere where they were happy also? As long as she could see them frequently, maybe she wouldn't have to leave Cestov.

"Where are you going next?" she asked softly.

"I promised that I would help you find your sister and then take you home. I am going wherever you go."

Tears sprang to her eyes. "I know you said that, but I'm sure you have responsibilities too. Don't you have a full load of cargo back there? Other than Tajka and her calves," she added hastily.

"I do. I'll see how much of it I can trade while we're here, but I won't take on any more items." He shrugged. "It's not the end of the world. We have sufficient financial reserves to be able to survive without new goods for an extended period of time."

"But what about your brother?"

The familiar shadow crossed his face. Every time the subject of his brother came up, he seemed so sad. The one thing that comforted her about her parting from Judith was that they had parted on good terms. Judith and Charlie had accompanied her to her car, Charlie giving her sloppy baby kisses while Judith ran down her usual list of things that Mariah should do before she stopped and laughed.

"I know you're far too old to need my advice," she had said. "I just can't seem to break the habit."

"I don't mind. I'm used to it. Nag."

"Brat." They had grinned at each other, then Judith hugged her and took Charlie back. "I'll see you in a couple of months?"

"I think so. After Detroit, I'll be in Austin for a while, but I should be back on the East coast by fall."

"Good. Maybe we can all go to the mountains for a few days when the leaves change."

"I'd like that. Love you, Ju."

"Love you too, Mariah."

Judith and Charlie had stood there and waved until she was out of sight. The memory brought a fresh lump to her throat. *I'm going to find you, Ju.*

"Maybe your brother will be here," she said softly now.

"I hope so. If nothing else, perhaps someone will have a record. After we land, I'll take you to that captain that Kwaret mentioned and see if he has any information on your sister. Perhaps he will know something about Bratan as well."

"I'm glad you're going with me."

"It is my honor."

He drew her closer and they both watched as the distant planet grew larger on the viewscreen.

FINDING CAPTAIN HREBEC PROVED MORE straightforward than anticipated. The *Defiance* had sent a communication ahead and almost as soon as they landed, the captain sent a message saying that he would meet with them. As Cestov escorted Mariah to a small office building on one side of the landing field, she found herself torn. As much as she hoped for news of her sister, locating Judith meant that she was that much closer to losing him.

Captain Hrebec was a large, older Cire with a commanding air. To Cestov's obvious annoyance, he addressed Mariah first.

"Are you safe? Do you need assistance?"

"Of course I'm safe," she said indignantly. "Why wouldn't I

be? But I do need your assistance with something. I'm trying to find my sister and nephew."

"You are not here against your will?" Hrebec cast a suspicious glance at Cestov.

"I would never keep a female against her will," he growled, wrapping his tail around her protectively.

She gave it a comforting pat. "I know you wouldn't. If anything, this is my fault. I chose to go onboard the Vedeckian ship in the first place. I knew it was risky, dangerous even, but luck was on my side and I found Kwaret, who introduced me to Cestov."

Hrebec hesitated, his gaze focused on her hand on Cestov's tail, then nodded. "I can see that the two of you have bonded. Please forgive me. It's just that..."

"Just what?" she asked.

Hrebec's tail whipped around behind him before he spoke. "Kwaret's suspicions were correct. It appears that Commander Khaen sold your relatives."

The world spun dizzily. Even though she had expected to hear the news, the shock still overwhelmed her. "Who did he sell them to? I have to find her and get her free."

Hrebec's tail lashed again as he looked at Cestov. "I am very sorry to have to tell you this. I did not think such a thing was possible, but it appears that she was purchased by a Cire."

"A Cire?" Cestov roared. "Who amongst us would do such a thing?"

Hrebec shook his head. "We don't know. The only information that I found in his records is that the purchaser was planning to take her to Granica."

"I've never heard of it. Where is it?" he growled. "Is it one of those decadent inner system worlds where such things are overlooked?"

"No." Hrebec consulted a small tablet. "It is a homestead

world. My understanding is that he was going to purchase a farm. There is a note in Khaen's records about farm labor."

"Farm labor? Judith?" Mariah gasped.

She imagined Judith as she saw her last, neatly dressed in khakis and a crisply ironed pink shirt. A choked laugh escaped her at the thought of her fastidious sister with her hands in the dirt, but she sobered rapidly as she thought of all the work that could be piled on those narrow shoulders.

"She's not cut out for physical labor. And what about Charlie? He's too young to work."

"Apparently that was somewhat of a sticking point in the negotiations." Hrebec said. "Khaen did not want to sell the child but the male insisted. I suspect Khaen must have been in a hurry because he ended up taking the deal, even though he didn't think he had been adequately paid."

"I have to go to Granica," she said urgently. "I have to rescue her."

"We will make plans as soon as we return to the *Wanderer*," Cestov promised, before turning back to Hrebec. "When the ship contacted you, did they tell you that I was searching for my brother also?"

"Yes, but I have no information about him. I'm sorry. I spoke to all of the Cires in our colony and no one was familiar with the name. I also checked with Chief Medic L'chong."

"A medic?" Cestov's shoulders tensed and she grabbed his hand. His tail came up to circle her wrist.

"Yes. He is a good friend of ours and he oversees many of the transients with medical issues. He has no record of him either."

Cestov's shoulders sagged with relief.

"Is it possible that he is using another name?" Hrebec asked gently. "I know that goes against our traditions, but perhaps, if he wished to hide…"

"No, he's not hiding from me. He left because we had a quarrel. I don't think he even thought I would come looking for him."

"But you did."

"Of course. I would have set out as soon as I found he was missing, but our ship was temporarily impounded, and it took over a week to get everything straightened out. By the time we were cleared to leave, the trail had gone cold. I have been looking for him ever since."

"I am very sorry." Hrebec looked thoughtful. "If you do not object, I still have some contact with the Council on Ciresia. I could ask them to post a message."

"A message?"

"Yes. Despite the Council's best efforts, many Cires have left Ciresia. They finally acknowledged that fact and opened a message board to allow for communication between those of us spread out across the galaxy."

"I don't know if he will have heard of it either, but I would be most grateful if you could arrange to have a message posted or let me know how to do so."

"Of course." Hrebec took down Cestov's information, then studied him thoughtfully. "You left Ciresia many years ago?"

"My father left when we were but children. My mother died from the Red Death and he couldn't stand to be without her. He had been a merchant on Ciresia, so he purchased this trading vessel and took us with him."

"You never had a home on another planet? Somewhere to which your brother might return?"

"Not really. Occasionally, our father would stay on a planet for a few months, usually to give us a chance to take some type of training, but I think being in one place only made him miss our mother more. Eventually, we would start traveling again."

"That sounds like a difficult life for a child," Hrebec said slowly.

Cestov shrugged. "It was all we really knew. I never minded. I didn't realize that Bratan did mind. Perhaps not at first but as the years wore on, it bothered him more and more. He tried to talk to me about it and I wouldn't listen. That is what led to our separation."

"I am truly sorry to hear that." Hrebec hesitated. "Would you both care to accompany me home? My mate is human and I'm sure that she would love to meet you, Mariah."

"Human?" Mariah asked.

"Yes." Hrebec smiled, his whole face alight with pride. "I now have two daughters and another child on the way. I never thought to have such happiness."

"You have a mate?" Cestov repeated, his face dazed. "But I thought we could only find that bond with a Cire female."

"As did I, but I am most definitely mated to my Abigail." He hesitated, glancing at Mariah. "And our species are capable of cross-breeding."

"What?" They both spoke in unison.

Her heart started to race. "Cestov, you told me—"

"I did not know. We were always told it was impossible."

"But that means I could be... pregnant." The world spun in a dizzying circle and only Cestov's arm kept her upright.

CESTOV MADE THEIR EXCUSES TO HREBEC AND HURRIED back to the *Wanderer*. Mariah still looked dazed and he alternated between joyous excitement and utter terror. He knew absolutely nothing about raising children, especially not ones who would be half-human. Mariah was so delicate; how much more so would an infant be? He shuddered, even as the thought of her swelling with his child sent a bolt of excitement straight to his cock.

If they did have a child, how could he ever let her go? And what if she didn't want to raise her child on a ship? He had not found his own childhood lacking but he had begun to wonder if perhaps there was something in Bratan's desire for a home and a family after all.

Mariah still had not spoken when he followed her into their cabin. Despite his anxiety, he couldn't help a swift, satisfied glance around at all the changes he had made to please her. The room seemed more like a home than ever before, although he knew that was more due to her presence rather than the colorful objects and soft fabrics he had added.

She walked to the bed and sat down, staring absently into space, and he followed her, kneeling in front of her to take her hands. "I'm so sorry, Mariah. I did not know."

"No, I know you didn't. I could see how shocked you were," she said, her voice distant and unnaturally calm.

"My miri, please talk to me."

"I don't know what to say," she said and then she started to laugh.

He didn't like the sound of her laughter and a minute later it turned to tears. To hell with this. He gathered her into his arms, rocking her as if she were a small child. He remembered the song she had sung to the slonga and hummed it as he moved. A long time later, her tears finally stopped, and she snuggled against him with a tired sigh.

"You sang to me."

"I did not know what else to do."

She wiped her eyes and gave him a watery smile. "I'm sorry. I don't usually break down like that."

"There is no need to apologize. I know that this has been a shock for you."

"And for you."

A shock, yes, but now that he had time to think beyond his concern for her, an overwhelmingly joyous shock.

"I know that this is difficult for you and I'm not sure what will happen, but I promise you, Mariah, I will do everything in my power to make sure that you and our child are happy and provided for in every way."

# CHAPTER FOURTEEN

Mariah asked for some time alone, and although he hated to leave her when she was so obviously upset, he decided the best thing he could do for her was to make preparations to depart as soon as possible for Granica. Perhaps finding her sister would make her happy.

Together he and Maldost traded a good part of their cargo, sacrificing profit for speed. Still, the cargo hold remained half-full once they were done. They both tacitly avoided discussing the slonga. As soon as they were through, he went to check with Plovac on the route to Granica.

"No more than a week," the navigator promised. "Perhaps less if you don't mind spending some extra fuel."

He was willing to do whatever it took to bring a smile back to Mariah's face.

"Yes, I want to arrive as quickly as possible. Are the items I requested on board?"

"Yes, sir."

"Very well. Prepare to depart but wait for my signal."

"Yes, sir." Plovac hesitated. "Is something wrong with Mistress Mariah?"

"Not exactly, but she has had some upsetting news."

"Please give her my best wishes."

"Thank you, Plovac," he said sincerely. His miri had won over his entire crew, even the solemn young navigator. "I'm sure that she will appreciate that."

He collected his packages and headed for their cabin - or was it still *their* cabin? Perhaps she would no longer wish to share it with him after his betrayal of her trust, no matter how unintentional. When he quietly opened the door, he found the room in darkness. His heart beat uncomfortably fast until he found her small figure curled in the center of the bed.

He approached quietly, unwilling to disturb her if she slept, but he caught the gleam of her eyes when she looked up at him.

"Do you wish to be alone?" he forced himself to ask. His tail was already trying to tug him closer to that dejected heap.

"No. I... I need you, Cestov," she whispered.

Her words unleashed his restraint and he slid into the bed, tucking her against him while his tail wrapped around her wrist. Having her back in his arms, her scent surrounding him, made his world complete again.

As soon as Cestov put his arms around her, something inside Mariah relaxed. His comforting, spicy scent surrounded her, and her troubled heart seemed lighter. As upset as she had been all afternoon, she had still found herself longing for his presence. She didn't—couldn't—blame him. The shock on his face had been completely genuine, but more than that, she believed to the bottom of her heart that he would never intentionally hurt her.

"I'm so sorry, my miri."

"It's not your fault. I chose to take the chance."

"Because you believed my words."

"Yes, but also because I didn't want any barriers between us," she admitted. She had wanted to feel every inch of his amazing cock. She gave a small laugh. "Judith started lecturing me about the use of condoms the day I started my period. As always, she was right."

"Would it ease your mind to talk to Hrebec's mate? Apparently, she has been in this position."

"No, I don't think so. He said they had three kids, so I suspect she's the maternal type—something I've never been. I never even played with dolls."

"We will learn together," he promised.

His words comforted her and yet...

"What are we going to do? If I'm pregnant, I can't go home." She reached up and stroked one of the ridges that arched back over his head. "I doubt that Earth is ready for a half-Cire child."

"You would leave me if that were an option?"

He looked so appalled that she pressed a quick kiss to his cheek.

"No, I would never take your child away from you." Especially when she knew what a precious gift it would be to him.

"We can adapt the ship to accommodate a child."

"Perhaps." The idea appealed to her. He could continue his travels while she and the baby accompanied him. And she had come to feel at home here. There was that word again. *Home.* Would it feel like a home to a child? "I guess we have some time to decide. We're still going to Granica, aren't we?"

"Of course. Unless..."

"Unless what?"

"Now that you may be in a delicate condition, perhaps you

would prefer to remain here? We do not know what we will encounter on Granica."

"I may be pregnant, not incapacitated. I am most certainly going with you," she said indignantly, but was mollified when he gave her a relieved sigh and pulled her closer.

"I confess, I am glad that you will accompany me. I would only worry if we were apart."

It hit her with a sudden blinding certainty that she did not want to be separated from him either and if she was pregnant, they would not be parting. She had always thought that she would feel trapped, tied down, by a husband and child, but this didn't feel that way. This felt... right.

"I don't know how Judith did it," she said thoughtfully as she snuggled against him.

"Did what?"

"Had a child on her own."

"Where is the father?"

"In a test tube." She laughed at his expression, already feeling lighter. "Have you heard of artificial insemination?"

"Using technology to create life? Yes." Sorrow flashed across his face. "My father said that many attempts were made on Ciresia, but none were successful. To know that we can breed successfully with another race..." His hand came down to cover her stomach. "It is a miracle for my people."

The feel of his big warm hand sent a streak of longing through her and she felt her body respond. His nostrils flared and he raised his head to look down at her as his tail moved from her waist to cup her breast.

"You are aroused, my miri."

"You seem to have that effect on me."

"I understand if you no longer wish to exchange pleasure with me."

"Oh, I wish." She gasped as his tail tugged lightly at a stiff peak. "But on the slim chance that I'm not pregnant, we should probably take some precautions. Even though I suspect worrying about birth control now is rather like locking the barn door after the horse is stolen."

He frowned, then nodded. "I believe I understand your idiom. I will speak to Whovian about additional precautions, although he will need to investigate. Few races practice such a thing anymore."

"Are you sure he's... capable?"

"Yes," he said thoughtfully. "I think he is. He has always been competent in that regard and the evenings when you sing to us have been good for him. He no longer rushes away to drink."

"He seems to be a very troubled male."

"Yes. Perhaps my initial instincts were correct after all." He rose over her. "But I no longer wish to discuss him. Even without precautions, I can still bring you to pleasure."

"But—"

Her protest was lost in his kiss as he proceeded to prove just how skilled he could be at satisfying her with his mouth, his hands, and that very naughty tail.

Cestov watched in satisfaction as Mariah drifted into sleep, exhausted by pleasure. His own cock throbbed and ached, but he had refused her offers to take him in her mouth. Guilt still consumed him that he had been so careless with her. However, as soon as she was asleep, he left the cabin in search of Whovian. He did not trust himself to be able to resist touching her for too long. He found the medic sitting in his lab, staring at an unopened bottle of Partallan liquor.

"Whovian? Is something wrong?"

"No more than normal." Before he could ask, Whovian shook his head. "Never mind. Can I assist you?"

"Yes. I need you to provide a birth control protocol for me."

"Birth control? An unusual concept in these times."

"Perhaps, but my ma—but Mariah has plans to return to Earth. That is if it's not already too late."

Even though he knew it was wrong, in his deepest heart he prayed that it was, in fact, too late. But that gave him an idea.

"Would you be able to tell if she was pregnant?"

Whovian's faced turned even whiter than normal and he shook his head rapidly. "No! I mean, no, probably not. I am unfamiliar with her species so I could not be sure about her hormonal patterns. I believe that you will need to let time provide your answer."

"I see. Does that mean that you cannot assist with birth control either?"

"No, that I can provide. Cire physiology is well-documented. Please have a seat." Whovian turned to his monitor and scrolled rapidly through a series of files that all looked like gibberish to Cestov. A few minutes later, he turned back to him. "This says that your seed is not fertile until you meet your mate. Is that not correct?"

"It is what I was always led to believe. Of course, I was always led to believe that only a female of my own species could be that mate."

"But you think that Mariah is your mate?"

*Yes.*

"I do not know. I want to share my life with her, but I have never mated before and I was too young to understand when my parents were still together."

"I see." Whovian flicked down the page. "You are attracted to her scent?"

"Yes, of course." Even thinking of her delicate fragrance caused his cock to stir.

"And your tail? Never mind, I have seen how often it is wrapped around her." Whovian hesitated. "Have you knotted?"

He wrestled with a wave of anger at having to discuss such an intimate matter. For all his faults, Whovian was a medic, after all.

"Yes," he said shortly.

"According to these records, you are most likely both mated and fertile."

Once again, delight and fear warred within him.

"Is it something you can prevent going forward?" If it wasn't already too late.

"Yes. It's a simple matter. I will take a sample of your blood and develop the formula. It will be ready tomorrow—no, make that this evening. Love can make any male do foolish things," Whovian said in a melancholy tone.

*Love?* The word echoed in his head and settled into place with a sense of inevitable rightness. Yes, he loved her. That first bloom of attraction had ripened into love.

"Perhaps you are right," he admitted.

"I will bring it to the lounge later this evening. Will Mariah feel like singing?"

"I believe she might," he said slowly. "It seems to give her comfort."

"That would be most enjoyable. She makes me forget..."

"Forget what?"

Whovian shook his head, the long red braids flying. "Many things."

Cestov did not press him to continue. Instead, he sat patiently while the medic took his samples and performed a few additional tests. By the time Whovian was through, he was ready to return to his mate. His *mate*. Another word that settled into his heart with sure knowledge.

Whovian's voice stopped him as he was about to leave.

"Thank you, Captain," he said quietly.

"For what, Whovian?"

"For rescuing me. For giving me a place to fight my battles." He looked at the bottle on the desk. "A battle that is not yet over but has been a little easier lately."

He nodded, embarrassed by the male's gratitude. "Do not be afraid to ask for help. We are a family, after all."

It wasn't until he stepped outside that he realized what he had said. What the hell was happening to him? Was he turning into the family man that he never thought he wanted to be—that he never thought he could be?

As if in response to his question, a small pink figure trotted up the corridor towards him, squealing happily.

"You found me, did you?" He picked up Lilat and settled her in the crook of his arm. "Was I gone too long today?"

She lifted her small trunk to his face as his tail came up to cover her. "Come on, little one. Let's see if my mate is awake. I bet she has missed you too."

## CHAPTER FIFTEEN

Mariah didn't sleep long, but when she awoke, she found that her anxiety had diminished. Not gone completely but settled into acceptance. Cestov was no longer beside her but she didn't panic the way she would have done if a potential human father had disappeared on her. Leaving aside the fact that it was his ship, she had absolutely no doubt that he would never desert her—her or their child.

A child. Her hand dropped to her stomach. What would she look like, she wondered. Would she have Cestov's green skin and dark eyes? And, oh lord, his tail? How did you put a diaper around a tail? She had never thought she wanted a baby but now she was seized by a fierce protectiveness.

She would be as good a mother to her baby as Judith had been to her.

*Judith.* Time to remember her main purpose here and tell Cestov that she was ready to depart for Granica as soon as possible. As she climbed out of bed, she saw several bundles wrapped in colorful fabrics on the end of the bed. Were they for her?

As she was debating peeking at one to see what it contained, the door opened and Cestov appeared, Lilat tucked against him, her small body looking even smaller against that massive chest. She had a sudden vision of him holding their child with that same protective hold and her eyes filled with tears. He might be an alien, but she couldn't imagine a better father.

"Oh, good. You're awake." He came closer and saw the tears in her eyes. "Is something wrong, my miri? I mean, is something else wrong?"

Lilat mewled anxiously.

"No, I was just thinking that I am lucky to have met you." Her smile was a little watery but genuine.

"Even under these circumstances? You honor me, Mariah."

He kissed her, slowly and sweetly, but she felt her body respond and she had to force herself not to cling to him when he lifted his head.

"I was just looking at these packages," she said breathlessly.

"Oh, good. They are for you."

"For me? Really?"

"Yes. It isn't much and I had to make some guesses, but I hope you will be pleased. Go ahead—open them," he urged as he sat down on the bed, still cradling Lilat. The slonga watched with her big dark eyes.

Feeling a little like a kid on Christmas morning, she unwrapped the first one. Shirts in several jewel tones spilled out, all soft to the touch and flowing over her hands like silk.

"These are beautiful."

"They will only compliment your beauty."

The second package contained pants, also in soft, flowing fabrics, and a garment that she assumed must be a nightgown since it was practically sheer.

"A dress for entertaining?" she asked innocently.

"Nightwear for my eyes only," he growled. "Although, I suspect it will not take me long to remove it."

"Umm, about that—"

"I just came back from seeing Whovian. He is making a birth control formula for me."

"For you?" she asked, shocked.

"Yes. He has sufficient documentation on Cire physiology to make the compound."

"On Earth, it always seems to be the woman who's responsible."

"A foolish notion. Are not two parties involved? Or perhaps three if you are like the Trojet."

"Generally, it is two." She peeped at him from under her lashes. Never had he looked more desirable than sitting there, cradling the small pink slonga tenderly against his big body. "How long will it take?"

"He said it would be ready tonight."

"That's good," she murmured, holding up the nightgown. "Very good."

The heat flared in his eyes and his tail darted towards her, but she skipped back out of reach. "Tonight, remember."

"Once again, callously rejecting me," he said solemnly, his eyes twinkling.

She rolled her eyes and opened the last two packages. The first one was a tablet of some kind.

"What is this?"

"It is a type of reader. You said you missed reading."

"That's very sweet of you, but I can't read your language." The translation device only appeared to work for verbal communication.

"I know. This will teach you Galactica, the standard trade language. It is designed to enhance learning and once you become fluent, there are a number of books available."

"Thank you," she said, trying not to cry again. But then she opened the fourth package and all hope was lost. It contained a small string instrument, similar to a dulcimer. Through her tears, she ran a finger across the strings delighting in the melodious notes.

"My miri, please do not cry. I thought that the dobron might make you happy." He placed Lilat carefully on the bed and drew her into his arms.

"These are happy tears. You are the most thoughtful man—male—I've ever met."

She kissed him again and as soon as his tongue touched hers, the taste of spice invading her mouth, she was lost. It wasn't until she heard an indignant squeal and felt a soft trunk patting her cheek demandingly that she came to her senses.

"Not now, Cestov. Tonight."

"Tonight," he echoed, then groaned as Lilat tried to climb back up on his lap and stepped on his massive erection. "It will be a very long evening."

Cestov lay in their bed, his eyes fixed impatiently on the door to the sanitary facility. The *Wanderer* was on her way to Granica and he found no small amount of satisfaction in having Mariah onboard with him. They had lifted off shortly before dusk and Plovac had managed to get them out of the system and on their way in time to join them for the evening session of music. When Mariah used his gift, plucking out a few notes on the dobron to accompany her song, he had been filled with satisfaction, delighted that he had found something to please her.

He hadn't pressed her to sing, concerned that she might prefer not to perform under the circumstances, but she had only smiled.

"Singing always makes me feel better."

"You are still concerned?"

"Concerned? Yes. It's not like I've ever done this before, even aside from the whole 'I'm in outer space with a huge, hunky alien' thing."

"My miri—"

She had pressed a finger to his lips. "I said concerned, not unhappy. This isn't perhaps what I bargained for, but if it had to happen, I'm happy that it was with you."

Words of love had rushed to his mouth, but he forced himself to remain silent. So many things were still unknown, and he did not want her to think that his protestations were simply in response to the child. The possible child, he reminded himself. They did not yet know if she bore his fruit.

His troubled thoughts were arrested by the sound of the door opening. She stood there, the translucent fabric of the nightgown rendered almost sheer with the light of the room behind her. It was everything he had hoped for when he had seen the garment behind the counter when he bought her other clothes. It had cost more than all of the rest of them put together, but he did not begrudge a single credit as she floated across the room to him with her graceful dancing steps. The fabric was so thin he could see every detail of her body, just slightly veiled in shimmering pink.

"I am speechless, my miri," he growled. Precum pearled on the tip of his cock and he grasped the wide base to stop himself from coming just at the sight of her.

"I assume that means you like it?" She twirled, the fabric floating out around her in a pink cloud.

"Yes." Words escaped him. He was reduced to a growing animal, only one thought on his mind—to bury himself in her sweet cunt as soon as possible. Thank Granthar that Whovian had handed him a small vial after the evening festivities and assured him that the formula would be effective immediately. "Come here."

"Right here?"

She settled down next to him a cloud of perfumed pink, but she was too far away. He dragged her closer, bending her back across his arm so that he could plunder her delicious mouth until she arched against him. He cupped her breasts, tugging eagerly at the taut peaks, while his tail tried to delve between her legs. The fabric was in his way, even though it had turned damp and transparent with her desire. Impatiently, he ripped it aside. Never mind the expense—he did not want anything between them.

"Cestov!" she cried out as the fabric tore. "What are you doing?"

"Preparing you for me."

He bent her farther back over his arm so that he had better access to those perfect breasts. The small peaks were already taut with excitement, but he wasn't satisfied. He devoted himself to them, licking and sucking until they were swollen and pink. As he held her in place for his attentions with one arm, he enlarged the hole he had made in the lower part of her gown so he could revel in the sweet, slick heat between her legs. He toyed with her pleasure button, bringing her close, then easing her back down as his tail played the same game, a teasing entry followed by a quick withdrawal.

Covered with her slickness, his tail explored farther down, finding the tight little rosebud of her bottom hole and probing at the delicate tissues. Her hands tightened on her shoulders and her body arched up against him as he slipped inside, but he felt the fresh rush of heat against his fingers.

"Please... I need to come."

"And you shall. But not until I am inside you."

He ripped away the remains of the garment and placed her on her hands and knees in front of him.

"So beautiful," he murmured, running his hand down the graceful curve of her back to the tempting roundness of her lush ass.

"Sweet talk later," she panted. "Sex now."

He could not resist. Clasping her hips, he entered her in a long hard stroke and they both cried out. He could feel her fluttering around him, and he used all of his self-control to maintain his position, to resist the urge to take her hard and fast. But she did not want his patience. Her soft buttocks pressed back against him in an urgent demand and he gave in to his need. Fire was already streaking down his spine, but he was determined that she would find her pleasure first. His tail went to her pleasure button, stroking and tugging as he gave in to his instincts, thrusting into her over and over, seeking to meld their bodies as one. He felt the heat rising, felt the base of his cock begin to swell, and he plunged as far as he could go into that heated embrace. His seed erupted in long shuddering pulses while she convulsed around him, calling out his name as he knotted deep inside her.

Too breathless for words, he collapsed onto the bed, rolling to his side and pulling her close against him, still embedded deep within her body. Another kind of home perhaps.

"Mmm," she said sleepily. "You ruined my nightgown."

"I do not regret it in the least. I only wish I had a thousand of them so I could rip a new one off of you every night."

Her body went still.

"Cestov, I still have to make sure that Judith and Charlie are safe and happy. That might mean returning to Earth."

A gaping hole appeared in his heart.

"You promised that you would never take my child from me."

"And I won't. But if I'm not pregnant, I need to think about them. Judith has given me so much. If she needs me on Earth, I have to stay. And even if she doesn't, I don't think I could go the rest of my life without seeing them."

"I feel that way about you, my miri."

She had her head buried in the covers and he cursed the knot that made it impossible for him to turn her to face him.

"I do too," she said quietly. "But you couldn't live on Earth."

"No. And even if your people would accept me, my government forbids all contact with pre-spaceflight worlds."

"We have spaceflight," she muttered.

"Beyond your solar system?"

"Well, no."

They lay together in silence until his cock finally softened enough for him to pull out. He immediately turned her to face him.

"Is that what you want, Mariah? To return to Earth?"

"No." Her hand came up to touch his cheek. "I would be happy to stay with you, travel on this ship, sing to your crew—but not unless I can still see my family as well."

He could not argue. He had spent the past five years searching for his brother because of that same bond.

"I do not want to be parted from you." It was the most he would allow himself to say.

"Nor I from you. And maybe it'll work out. Maybe she's found a happy home and we can visit her whenever we want. Just like I used to do."

"I hope so."

But even though she snuggled closer and buried her head in his chest, he already felt the distance between them.

## CHAPTER SIXTEEN

Four days later, Mariah woke up alone. It had been an odd week. There were times when everything seemed perfect and she and Cestov could relax and enjoy each other's company. But there had been other times when she could feel the distance between them. Her heart was torn in two different directions, even though she told herself not to borrow trouble. The odds were good that she was pregnant, and, in that case, there was no decision to be made. She wouldn't take his child away from him no matter what. She could only hope that Judith would agree to remain with her.

Her attempt at serenity lasted until she visited the bathroom. Her period had started. She looked down at the small smear of red and burst into tears. In that second, she realized just how much she had wanted to be pregnant. Not to make her decision easier but because she wanted to have a baby. With Cestov. With the male she loved. The truth broke over her like a wave and she cried harder. She loved him, loved his sweet, protective nature, loved his kindness and the sly twinkle in his eyes when he teased her. She loved the way he wrapped her in his big body as if he couldn't stand to be without her. She even loved the tail that always wanted to touch her.

She wanted to tell him how she felt but it wouldn't be fair to him. No matter how much she loved him, she had to be prepared to look after her sister—because that's what family did. They sacrificed in order to make you happy. Judith had sacrificed for her. Now it was her turn.

She emerged from the bathroom to find Cestov waiting for her.

"I have good news. It appears that we will be landing on Granica within a few—" He broke off abruptly as he saw her face. "My miri, what is wrong?"

"I'm not p-pregnant."

No matter how hard she tried, she couldn't control her trembling lips, and her attempt to form a smile was a pitiful effort. He looked just as devastated, but he stepped forward and drew her into the comfort of his embrace.

"I am so sorry." His arms tightened. "But I should have known that it was too good to be true. My people are destined to come to an end. It was foolish of me to get my hopes up."

The desolation in his tone penetrated her own sorrow. "Hrebec said it was possible. He said he had a baby with his human mate."

"A miracle, perhaps?" He put a finger under her chin and raised her face to his. "I had very much wanted to share this experience with you, but perhaps this will make your choices easier."

He looked so sincere, and so sad, that her heart physically ached. "No, Cestov, it doesn't. I didn't want to leave you before and I don't want to leave you now. My fondest wish is that we can find Judith and Charlie and that they will want to stay with us." She finally managed a smile. "Although, we may need a bigger ship."

"I will arrange to get a larger ship," he said immediately.

*So sweet.*

"But I don't know what she's been through. If her life has been... difficult, then she may want only to return to Earth."

"I know. You must do as you feel best. But first we must find her. I was coming to tell you that we should be landing within a few hours."

Butterflies fluttered in her stomach. Was she finally close to finding them?

"Do you still think we should start with Selo?" she asked.

In Cestov's research about Granica, he had found that it was primarily an agricultural planet. There was a large interstellar port on the main continent, but since his ship was small enough to land almost anywhere on the surface, they didn't have to start their search there. From the information on the interwebs, it appeared that most of the new settlements were concentrated on the northern part of the continent, and Selo was the central town in that area.

"Yes, I think so. Many of the new residents appear to be settling near there. I hope that will make it easier to find news of your sister. Or the Cire who bought her," he said grimly. "He has much to answer for."

"We have to make sure Judith and Charlie are safe first."

"Of course." He rubbed his chin. "I thought perhaps it would be best to send Maldost into town to investigate."

"Maldost. Really?" she asked doubtfully. As much as she had grown to like the big male, she still thought of him as an impetuous youth.

"Yes. I believe he can handle the responsibility—and he has a way with people. If I start making inquiries, people may assume that I am like the Cire who bought her."

"I could go," she offered.

"Absolutely not. I will not permit you to go without my

protection. You are too desirable." His eyes heated and despite her sadness, she felt her body respond.

"You're going to have to wait a few more days for that. I just started my period."

He frowned. "Your what?"

"My menstrual cycle?"

He still looked blank, so she patted his arm. "Never mind. It just means that we can't have sex for a few days. And that I need to go see Whovian."

"What is wrong? Are you ill?" His nostrils flared. "I do not understand. Your scent has changed. It is deeper, richer, more intoxicating. But I also detect a hint of blood. Are you injured?"

"No, Cestov. I promise I'm fine. But I do need to talk to him about supplies."

"I will escort you."

The thought of having to try and explain her requirements in front of both of them made her cringe. "Uh, why don't you go and brief Maldost instead? Then I'll go get Lilat and come find you." If they didn't go and get the calf every morning, she would come looking for them.

He reluctantly agreed and a short time later, she was standing in Whovian's lab trying to explain what she wanted. To her enormous relief, he was familiar with the concept of menstrual cycles and after a few moments thought, he produced a small concave white disk.

"What's that?" she said suspiciously.

"It is a type of sponge. It will absorb your flow and process it."

"How long does it last?"

"It will absorb—" he stopped to calculate "—one-tenth of your body weight."

"Does that mean I don't need to change it?"

"Not until you have ceased your flow. Then remove it and

leave it to dry for at least two days. You can reuse it on your next cycle."

She winced. "Won't it be, umm, kind of nasty?"

He looked horrified. "Of course not. It will appear just as it does now. I told you that it will process your blood—it will absorb and cleanse it."

A little uncertainly, she reached out and took it. One? For her whole period? Since she didn't have much choice, she would give it a try. As she studied it, she realized that it actually resembled a diaphragm, which made her wonder...

"Umm..." She twisted her hands before finally blurting out. "Is it okay to have sex while wearing it?"

To her great relief, he didn't even blink. "Yes, it is quite safe."

"Thank you, Whovian."

He bowed his head. "If I can be of some small assistance to you, I am very grateful. Your songs have made my sorrow much easier to bear."

"Sorrow?" she asked softly.

His eyes turned distant and for a moment, she thought he was about to speak. But in the end, he only shook his head.

"It is my burden. Just know that you have made it lighter."

"I'm glad. Thank you for telling me. And thank you for this."

"Do you need further instructions?"

"No, no. That's fine," she said quickly. "I'll come back if I do."

A short time later, she and Lilat joined Cestov on the bridge. Granica was coming into view. Unlike Trevelor, it looked distinctly alien with landmasses in shades of purple while the seas were soft shades of pink.

"Look, Lilat," she said. "It matches your colors."

The slonga didn't seem interested. She was too busy using

her trunk to explore Mariah's hair, something she had developed a fascination with over the past couple of days. Mariah wondered if it was because of the pink streaks, fading now. Did any of these planets have salons?

Maldost bounced over to her, although perhaps bounce was not quite the right term for seven feet of furred male. He still sometimes reminded her of an oversized puppy.

"I'm going to find your sister," he said confidently.

"Thank you, Maldost. I really hope you can."

"Does she look like you? Pale and almost bald?"

She choked back an indignant protest. Her long hair was one of her favorite features, but then she supposed that compared to Maldost, she must appear pretty bare.

"Even balder," she said solemnly, remembering Judith's short bob. "Or at least she was. Her hair may have grown by now."

"To this length?" He started to reach for the ends of her hair and Cestov grabbed his hand with a low growl.

"You do not touch her hair."

"No, no. Sorry, boss." Maldost's ears went down but he gave Mariah a quick wink when Cestov stepped back.

"Just be... careful, all right?" she asked. "If she's in a bad situation, I don't want to make it worse."

His golden eyes turned serious. "I will be careful. You can rely on me."

"I know I can. Thank you."

THE LANDING WENT AS PLANNED AND THEY PARKED THE *Wanderer* on the small field at one end of the town. While they waited for Maldost to return, she and Cestov went through the images the ship had taken during the descent. The landscape was sparser than she had expected, despite the soft colors.

Most of the surface appeared to be covered with low-lying vegetation in various shades of purple with taller plants only near the pink lakes. They had flown over several small homesteads, most of them consisting of a few one-story buildings and large herds of robedas—a type of long-haired cattle that looked rather like small furred rhinoceros—before landing on a small plateau that spread in gently rolling hills towards a distant mountain range.

Cestov also showed her how to use the ship's viewport to observe the town in greater detail. It was composed of more low buildings spread out along a long main street. The buildings were primarily formed from what looked like pink stucco and they reminded her of the adobe buildings she had seen in New Mexico, down to the open patios and courtyards that fronted many of them. Under other circumstances, she would have enjoyed having a chance to explore. A number of different species roamed the streets, but the most predominant were the native Granicans, a race of small, slender people with creamy pink skin and cotton candy hair in a variety of shades.

It all looked peaceful and pleasant, and she could only hope that her sister's life here had turned out to be the same.

Despite a number of automated wagons, the most common mode of transportation appeared to be the xuths, tall shaggy beasts that bore an uncanny resemblance to Earth camels—aside from the fact that they had four eyes and their long shaggy fur was a dusty blue. However, they had the two humps, and most carried a saddle between those humps. She watched in amusement as a small boy ordered one to its knees, then climbed aboard with a regal air. Would Charlie have done that someday?

Her eyes filled with tears, and Cestov came over to put his arms around her.

"What is it, my miri?"

"Just thinking about Charlie. I hope he's all right. That they both are. This doesn't seem like a bad place, does it?"

"No," he said slowly. "But I do not like the presence of Dhalecs."

"Of what?"

"The large blue males." He pointed out two of the different aliens she had noticed. Big, hulking males with no necks and massive tusks, they didn't seem to be doing anything particularly harmful despite their forbidding appearance. They were seated in an outdoor patio in front of what appeared to be a tavern, drinking from large mugs.

"They aren't bothering anyone."

"No. But they do not have a good reputation. They are mercenaries and they work for whoever will pay the most. Which is not necessarily bad, but they do have a reputation for somewhat... unscrupulous behavior. It just seems like an odd place to find them."

He glanced down at her worried face and smiled reassuringly. "I'm sure it is nothing. My father was somewhat paranoid about other species and I suppose he has passed that on to me."

"He did? Everyone on your ship comes from somewhere different."

He laughed. "You are correct. It is probably more accurate to say that he passed on his feelings about a few specific races such as the Vedeckians and the Dhalecs. He had strong opinions about what was right and what was wrong, and they violated his moral code." His smile faded. "I think he might have been disappointed by some of the choices I have made."

"I don't believe you would ever do anything morally wrong," she said immediately. Oh, she could believe that he might not follow every regulation to the letter or always behave with perfect propriety, but she knew he would never deliberately set out to hurt someone else or to take advantage of them.

"Thank you, Mariah." He tugged her closer and together they continued to watch the street.

Now that he had called her attention to them, she kept her eyes on the two Dhalecs. She began to notice that most of the other people in town avoided them. Twice, someone would start to enter the courtyard where they were drinking, spot the males, and move away. When a young Granican male came to bring them more drinks, his hands shook so badly that she could see the tray moving. The Dhalecs grabbed the mugs and sent him off with a casual cuff to the back of his head.

She began to suspect that Cestov's father had been right. They were not nice people.

But then she spied Maldost approaching from the alley behind the main street and all thoughts of the Dhalecs disappeared.

"He's coming. Let's go meet him."

"Not too fast, my miri. You will injure yourself," Cestov said as she tripped over the leg of her chair in her haste.

"I'm fine, I'm fine. Let's go."

She tugged impatiently on his hand and he laughed and gave in. When Maldost emerged from the lift, they were waiting for him.

"Did you find her?" she burst out.

"I'm not sure—but perhaps."

## CHAPTER SEVENTEEN

Mariah stared at Maldost and tried to refrain from shaking him. "What do you mean you're not sure?"

He shook his head and led the way to the lounge. "Just a minute. I'm hungry."

"Maldost, you're killing me here. What happened?"

"Patience, my miri," Cestov said soothingly.

Together they waited for Maldost to retrieve an enormous bowl of food from one of the cooking machines.

"Well?" she demanded as soon as he sat down.

He frowned. "No one in this place wants to talk much. I did the usual—browsed through some merchant stalls, stopped for some food, tried to strike up a conversation with anyone I met." He shook his head. "Usually people in an isolated trading town are eager to talk to strangers. These people seemed reluctant to talk about anything other than business."

"Did you see the Dhalecs?" Cestov said grimly.

"No, but I heard enough whispers to guess that they were here."

"What about my sister?" she interrupted.

"I started a few conversations about strange new species—sorry, Mariah—but as soon as I even hinted at someone remotely human, they stopped talking." He looked at her, worry in his eyes. "Which I suspect means trouble."

"Oh no." Her heart started to pound. "Did you find any?"

"No, not really. Just that odd reluctance to talk." He looked at Cestov. "And they were even worse if I mentioned a Cire."

"So, you didn't find out anything?" Her hopes started to slip away.

"No, but I was on my way back to the ship when one of the Granicans beckoned me into an alley. He gave me this." He held out a scrap of paper with some numbers on it.

"What are those? I don't understand."

"They are coordinates," Cestov said. "Did he say anything else?"

"No. He shoved it into my hand and told me to go. Then he vanished."

"Do you think that's where my sister is?" she asked Cestov, who was frowning at the piece of paper.

"I don't know. But I think we need to go and find out."

AFTER CONSIDERING THE MATTER, CESTOV DECIDED THAT the best approach would not be to try and land the *Wanderer* at the given coordinates. If there was trouble there, he did not want the sight of the ship to trigger any kind of incident.

"I think it would be best to approach like normal travelers," he said. "Could you procure transportation, Maldost?"

"Of course. Do you want two of the riding beasts?" He grinned, showing his large white fangs.

"I think we would prefer one of the wagons."

As soon as Maldost left, he turned to his mate. She had been cycling between excitement and fear, delighted that it appeared her sister was so near, and terrified of what she would find.

"Perhaps you should stay on the ship," he told her.

"Absolutely not. I'm going with you."

There was nothing he wanted more. Even now, his tail slid across the small space between them and wrapped around her ankle. But...

"We do not know what we are facing. It could be dangerous."

"If my sister is there and it's dangerous, then there's all the more reason why I need to go."

"You cannot protect yourself."

She bared her small white teeth in an adorable attempt to look ferocious.

"You bet I can, buddy. If you won't give me one of those gun things, I'll find one somewhere."

"You'll be safer here on the ship," he suggested, even though he hated the thought of being parted from her. "If I find your sister, I promise I will bring her to you."

"And what if something happened to you?" Tears filled those big blue eyes. "Then I'll have lost three people that I lo... care for. And I would never know what had happened to any of you."

His instincts vied with each other—the urge to protect her at all cost with the urge to have her with him at all times—but in the end, her tears won him over. He could not stand to see her so unhappy.

"You are a most infuriating female," he said with a sigh.

"Does that mean you'll take me with you?"

"Yes."

Her smile blinded him. "Thank you, Cestov."

While Maldost was arranging to hire a wagon, Cestov instructed Plovac to move the *Wanderer* about halfway to their destination. They would still be far enough away to avoid detection and Maldost would meet them there so they could go the rest of the way in the local vehicle.

Unfortunately, Mariah did not handle the wait well. She paced back and forth, coming up with increasingly dire speculations.

There was only one way he could think of to calm her down. "Come with me."

"But what if Maldost comes back? I want to be ready to go."

"It's going to take him at least an hour to get here." He picked her up and carried her off to their cabin as she sighed and stopped protesting.

"What are you going to do? If you think I'm going to take a nap, you're crazy."

"No, my miri, I have a better plan."

"You do?"

"Yes. Here." He handed her the box he had retrieved from the cargo hold.

"What's this?"

"Open it and find out."

She frowned but opened the box, then gasped in surprise. "Oh, these are gorgeous."

The box was filled with thin silk scarves in a vibrant array of colors.

"Where did they come from?"

"They are part of the trade goods." An expensive part because they were made from the finest fibers spun by the spiders of Wignow, but he had decided that he would rather see them on his mate than worry about his profits.

"And they're for me?"

He nodded and she threw herself into his arms. "You are really the sweetest male."

After kissing her until her firm little nipples rubbed against his chest, he lifted his head and smiled down at her.

"Perhaps I am not entirely sweet. I must admit that I had something in mind."

"In mind? With the scarves?"

"Yes. That very first night, you promised to show me the dance of the seven veils." The idea had taunted him ever since.

"You know I don't remember that."

"I do."

"And I'm not even sure it's a real dance—it's just something I've heard people say," she protested, but he could see that she was considering the idea.

"Dance for me, my miri. Please."

"I suppose I can give it a try." She ran a teasing hand along the heavy ache of his erect shaft. "I'm sure there's a sultan in the story. Are you going to play that part?"

"A sultan?"

"A rich man. A ruler. One who would be lounging on a bed of pillows while his female danced for him. Can you be my sultan?" With an impish grin, she disappeared into the sanitary facility with her box of scarves.

A rich ruler? Not a role he ever expected to play, but the least he could do was join in her game. He willingly stripped out of his clothes and went to the bed, piling up as many pillows as he could find. The thought of her dancing for him, clad only in the thin scarves, had his seed pearling on the tip of his erection. He gave it a rough stroke, willing himself to be patient. The door opened a moment later and he had to grip the base of his shaft to prevent himself from exploding.

Three scarves fluttered around her lush hips while another two barely contained her full breasts. The final two veiled her head, leaving only her eyes visible—big, blue, and mysterious. Singing softly, she danced around the room, as graceful as ever but with a seductive edge that had his cock throbbing in his hand as he desperately gripped the base.

One veil slipped away, then another, leaving only a thin cloud of blue covering her luscious cunt. The translucent fabric barely concealed anything, yet he found himself as anxious for her to remove it as if it had been entirely opaque. He wanted her completely bared to him. The next scarf came from around her breasts, flashing a tantalizing hint of pointed pink nipples.

"Mariah," he groaned.

She only smiled at him and kept dancing, singing something about pouring sugar. He didn't care; he just wanted her to keep dancing, to keep revealing herself to him. Another veil and her breasts sprang free, naked and perfect, undulating with her movements, and then the final one fluttered to the floor.

He could wait no longer. Forgetting his role, he sprang from the bed to take her in his arms. The last two veils still covered her head and he ripped them away, wanting to see her beautiful face as he kissed her. More seed gathered on the head of his cock as he carried her to the bed, sliding a thick finger between her folds, praying that she was ready for him. Thank Granthar. She was slick and hot and perfect. He could wait no longer. He slid into her as she arched up into his thrust.

"Yes, my sultan. Yes, Cestov."

He plunged helplessly, overwhelmed by his need for her, and she met every stroke, her soft cries urging him on until he exploded in shuddering waves as his cock swelled, knotting inside her. His tail flicked across her clit and then she was coming too, in exquisite little pulses that sent jolts of pleasure through his body.

He collapsed onto the bed and pulled her close, careful not to disturb their joined bodies.

"I like this dance very much."

"I could tell." She smiled up at him and put her hand on his cheek. "Thank you."

"For what?"

"For the scarves, for playing with me, for being here with me."

"If it is possible, I will always be with you."

Her eyes filled with tears and she buried her face in his chest.

"Please let it be possible," he heard her whisper.

## CHAPTER EIGHTEEN

Cestov slowed the wagon as they approached the ranch. It looked like all of the other buildings they had flown over, although perhaps a little more run down. The wall that surrounded the outer courtyard could have used painting and a line of flowering bushes along the wall drooped, half-dead from lack of care. They had seen a herd of robedas in a nearby field but there didn't seem to be anyone taking care of them. Even the air seemed curiously still.

"Where is everyone? Wouldn't you think a place this size would have people working here?" Mariah whispered.

"Yes," he said grimly and put his hand on his weapon. He should never have let her come with him. Even though he didn't spot any obvious danger, he couldn't help but wonder if something lurked in the silent shadows.

"I guess I'm just being silly," she said firmly. "After all, it's just a house, right?"

Despite her words, she shrank a little closer to him and his tail gave her a comforting hug.

"Do not worry, my miri. I'm sure everything is fine."

He brought the wagon to a halt outside the courtyard gate. "Perhaps you should wait here."

Her eyes narrowed. "Why?"

"If it is the home of a Cire, he might be more receptive to seeing me alone than he would be to admit a couple."

"And if he's a horrible slave owner, he might think you're the same and relax," she pointed out.

"Perhaps you have a point." And he would rather have her close at hand.

"All right," he agreed. "Just stay behind me."

Mariah rolled her eyes but nodded and fell into place behind him. His tail reached back and curved around her wrist and she gave it a grateful pat. She wasn't nervous exactly, but the absolute silence was definitely strange. She could hear the distant lowing of the cattle, but the faint rustle of the wind was the only other sound. If this were a western movie, she would have expected to see a tumbleweed roll by.

Cestov pushed open the gate, the hinge creaking loudly enough to make her jump. Inside the wall, the courtyard had the same abandoned air. More dying flowers lined the edge of an open veranda on one side and an ornate sundial had been knocked off its pedestal. The tile path that led to the front door was covered with dust and scuffed footprints. Her hopes began to fade again. Surely her sister wasn't here? She couldn't imagine Judith living in such an untidy environment. But then her eye caught on a flash of red beneath the bushes.

She tugged on Cestov's tail and pointed. A brightly colored ball, obviously a child's toy, lay half-concealed in the vegetation. He saw it and nodded, his hand tightening over his weapon. *Please*, she prayed, *please let them be here.*

The path led up to the veranda and a large set of forbidding double doors, strapped with metal. A small bell hung next to them. Gesturing for her to stay to one side, Cestov pulled on the bell. The unexpectedly melodious chimes rang through the courtyard, at odds with the oppressive silence. They waited, but nothing stirred within the house. After a long pause, he knocked on the door, his fist thudding loudly.

"Go away. I already told you I don't know where the papers are located."

The voice was undoubtedly feminine, but young and frightened. Not her sister. Her heart sank but she couldn't help responding to the terror in the soft voice.

"We're not here looking for papers. We're trying to find someone. Can you help us?" She took another look around the abandoned courtyard. "Or do you need help?"

Another long silence and she began to despair of any response, but then she heard the sound of a bolt being unfastened. The door cracked open. A pretty young Granican with lavender hair stood there, her shaking hands holding a gun as she stared at them. Her gaze traveled from Mariah to Cestov and her eyes widened as the color drained from her face.

"Who are you?" she whispered.

As she spoke a small blond head appeared around the edge of her skirt. The little boy never even glanced at Mariah but looked straight at Cestov.

"Daddy!" he cried and burst into tears as he threw himself at her mate.

Cestov instinctively opened his arms and picked up the young human. The little boy sobbed against his neck and he gave Mariah a helpless look. She stared at the two of them and he saw the moment she reached the same conclusion he had just reached. His brother—his twin brother—was the despicable Cire who had bought a human female as a slave.

His shock and grief overwhelmed him. How could Bratan have done such a thing? The brother he remembered would never have violated such a fundamental tenet of their society—but more than that, he was a genuinely kind male, always ready with a friendly word or a helping hand. How could he have sunk so low? And if he had, Cestov could only blame himself. How much Bratan must have changed since he left their ship, all because Cestov hadn't had the ability to understand his brother's dreams. His self-loathing was so great that it took him a minute to realize the boy was speaking to him.

"Where you been, Daddy? Devi said you was never coming back."

The boy scowled at the young girl, who was still staring at Cestov as if she'd seen a ghost. No wonder, if she thought he was Bratan. But where was his brother? Had he compounded his sins by abandoning his slaves in this desolate location? He couldn't—wouldn't—believe it, but the alternative was even more painful. His heart ached and he hugged the little boy closer.

"Charlie. Charlie, do you remember me?" Mariah said urgently.

The little boy shook his head and buried a wet face back in Cestov's neck.

"Devi—is that your name?" Cestov asked.

"Devoji," she corrected, still staring.

"Where is my brother? Where is Bratan?"

"Your brother?" She swayed a little on the doorstep and Mariah reached for her. The young girl turned to thank her, and her mouth dropped open as she took a second look. "You—you're related to Mistress Judith, aren't you?"

"Yes, I am. She's my sister. Can you tell me where to find her?"

"I... I think you'd better come in."

Devoji led the way into the house and they both followed. The boy was still clinging to his neck, his small arms almost strangling him, and his tail came up to pat his back soothingly. Inside, all the windows were shuttered, but he could see well enough to notice that the house was in much better condition than the outside, sparsely furnished but clean and well-tended.

"Where is he?" he demanded as soon as the door shut behind him. "Where is my brother?"

"And my sister?"

Mariah stood next to him, her hand on Charlie's small back. The little boy finally raised his head and looked at her.

"You look like Mama."

"Yes, I do. That's because we're sisters. I knew you when you were just a baby."

"Not a baby. I'm a big boy."

"Yes, you are. So big." Her eyes filled with tears. "Did your mama ever mention me? My name is Mariah."

He tilted his head, considering her. "You's the singing one?"

"Yes, that's right. I used to sing to you, too."

"Sing for me," he demanded.

"I will, but first we need to talk to Devoji."

Mariah's eyes flicked up to meet his and he saw the same dread that filled his heart in hers. If what he suspected was true, Charlie didn't need to hear the discussion.

"Charlie, can you show Mariah your room?" he asked.

"No." Charlie's arms went back around his neck. "Don't wanna leave you, Daddy."

"Why don't the two of you go?" Mariah said softly. "I'll talk to Devoji."

"You should not be alone, my miri." He couldn't stand the thought her hearing the news he dreaded alone.

"I'll be fine—"

A baby cried. The sound echoed through the silent house and Devoji jumped.

"I'll just go get her," she said in a rush and disappeared through a passageway at the back of the room while they stared at each other.

Mariah frowned. "She looks too young to have a baby."

"Not Devi's baby." Charlie scowled at them. "My baby."

"Your baby?"

"That's what he says." Devoji smiled as she came back into the room holding a tiny bundle swathed in blankets. "This is his sister, Claire."

Mariah's eyes filled with tears. "That's my middle name. Can I hold her?"

"She don't take much to strangers..." Devoji began, then went silent as Mariah reached for the baby.

As she picked her up, he watched in shock as a small green tail emerged from the blanket and curled around Mariah's wrist. She looked down at the baby and turned to him so he could see. The baby was completely and indisputably part Cire.

As Mariah gathered the baby into her arms, her heart swelled with emotion. The pale green skin and tiny little tail were undoubtedly Cire, but those big blue eyes looking up at her so seriously—they were her sister's eyes, her own eyes.

"Hello, little one," she whispered, even as the tears began to fall. There was no force in the universe that would have caused her sister to leave her baby behind. She looked up at Devoji and said softly, "She's gone, isn't she?"

The girl nodded, tears in her own eyes. "Not long after the baby was born. She caught a fever, but she kept saying she was fine, and we were all so worried about the other business that we didn't realize just how sick she really was. When Master Bratan figured it out, he took off for town with her." She glanced at Charlie, then dropped her voice. "He never made it. They were ambushed somewhere on the road."

"Ambushed?"

"They found the wagon overturned on the side of the road. Marshal Zakon tried to say it was an accident because Master Bratan was driving too fast, but he drove that thing like it was a part of him. I know it wasn't an accident. Especially when the Dhalecs started showing up."

"The Dhalecs?" Cestov had joined them, although she noticed he had his hand covering Charlie's ear as he cradled him against his body. The little boy watched her thoughtfully, his thumb in his mouth.

"Yes," Devoji said. "They want the ownership papers for the ranch."

"Where are the papers?"

"I don't know, but they told me to find them or they'd start searching."

Mariah looked at the young girl, remembering the monstrous aliens she had seen in town. "I'm very impressed you stood up to them."

"Well, the first time my brothers were here—and I have a lot of brothers." She flashed a quick smile. "A lot of relatives really, and so far, the Dhalecs haven't out and out threatened anyone. Even though we all know it's coming. They've been back twice but someone has always been with me. Today, my brother Devorat had to go help with our family's harvest and won't be back until tonight. When I heard the bell, I thought it was them."

"But you really don't know where these papers are?"

"No." Devoji shook her head again and then looked as Cestov. "But I know what they say. He left the ranch to you."

## CHAPTER NINETEEN

"He doesn't want it," Mariah said automatically. They had never even discussed the possibility of settling down in one place. What they needed to do was to get these children far away from this dreadful place. The baby in her arms cooed and she smiled down at that sweet, non-human face. There was no question of returning to Earth now. But no matter the circumstances of her birth, this was her niece and she was going to make sure she never doubted that she was loved.

"Just a minute, my miri," Cestov said.

"What? You don't honestly want to stay here? After everything that has happened?" She shuddered to think of what Judith had been through, sold to an alien who appeared to be nothing like his brother. Forced to have a child...

"I do not know what happened," he said slowly. "And I want to find out."

He looked down at Charlie, half-asleep now as he sucked on his thumb and nestled against Cestov with every appearance of contentment. Maybe his brother had been good to the child, she decided, but it didn't excuse his treatment of her sister.

"He was my brother, Mariah," he continued. "I owe that to him."

"Owe him? After he fuc—freaking bought my sister to be his slave?"

"What?" Devoji looked shocked. "I do not believe you. I have never seen a couple more in love."

"Love?" she snorted. "Somehow I doubt that."

Anger surged through her veins and even though she suspected that it was partially a response to her grief, she welcomed the fiery burn.

"When will your brother return, Devoji?" Cestov asked.

"Late this afternoon. He said he would be back in time to milk the robedas." She nodded at Claire. "The little one has taken quite well to their milk."

Her throat threatened to clog with tears. "How long has it been?"

"Just over a month now." Sadness crossed the girl's face. "My oldest brother sent a message to Ciresia to try and contact you, but we hadn't heard anything yet. Devorat was Bratan's foreman so he's been taking care of the herds. I've been staying here so that the house is occupied—and to make it easier for Charlie."

Mariah looked at her nephew again, fully asleep now, his body sprawled against Cestov's with the easy confidence of a child who has no fear that he will be harmed. In spite of her rush to leave, she understood Devoji's point. Maybe it would be easier for Charlie to have a chance to get to know them both. She sighed.

"Why don't you put him to bed and then we can talk?" she asked Cestov.

He hesitated, seeming reluctant to part with her nephew,

but then he nodded. "Where is his room?"

"This way."

Devoji led the way down the long hallway and Mariah followed along. One side of the wide corridor had windows that would open onto the courtyard, although they were all shuttered now, with rooms lining the other side.

"This is my room," the girl said as they passed the first door. "That is, if you wish for me to stay..."

"Yes."

"Yes."

They both spoke at the same time, then Mariah added, "Please."

During the time she'd spent with Judith and Charlie, she had always been the aunt, not the mother, and she wasn't at all sure what to do with both an infant and a toddler.

"Of course," Devoji said with a warm smile. "I would hate to leave the little ones. And this is Charlie's room."

She opened the second door and Mariah almost burst into tears again. The room was a sparser version of Charlie's room at home. She still remembered Judith fussing about the right shade of blue and carefully hand-painting the train border—the same border that ran around the top of these walls.

Cestov carefully lowered Charlie into the little bed, his tail lingering as if reluctant to part from the little boy before he stepped away.

"Would you like to see the rest of the house?" Devoji said softly as she pulled the door half-shut.

"Yes, please." Would there be other signs of Judith's presence?

There were. Claire's room was decorated in pale yellow with another hand-painted border. Another design she remembered Judith discussing with her, even though she had thought it rather silly at the time.

The master bedroom was the worst. A huge bed, heaped with pillows—not quite as many as Judith had liked at home, but enough to show the unmistakable stamp her sister had put on the room. Curtains in Judith's favorite soft green draped the windows and there was even a small dressing table. Could she possibly have misjudged Cestov's brother? It didn't seem like the room of a slave; it looked like the room of a woman with an indulgent husband. She wandered over to the dressing table, and this time there was no restraining her tears. The woven friendship bracelet that matched her own was lying next to a wooden brush.

"Hush, my miri," Cestov's arms came around her. "You are upsetting the little one."

"I... I can't..."

"I'll take her," Devoji said quickly. "You two take some time."

As soon as the girl left the room, Cestov picked her up and carried her over to the big chair in the corner, cradling her in her arms as she sobbed. When her cries finally died down, she looked up to see that his eyes were wet with tears too.

"We were too late," she said.

"I know. How can I ever forgive myself?"

"He was the one who left you."

"Because I did not listen to what he wanted. Because I thought it was a foolish, impossible dream. He wanted a mate and I thought such a thing could never be. Yet, now I have you and now I know it's possible." His eyes closed for a moment. "At least he had a chance to discover that for himself."

"You mean he had the chance to buy a mate," she said bitterly.

"Stop that, Mariah. Have you seen anything in this house that indicates your sister was a slave to him?"

"Maybe he was a nice slave owner," she muttered resentfully.

"You are forgetting something else."

"What?"

"Claire. Bratan would not have been able to get her pregnant unless he became fertile, and he would only have become fertile if he had found his mate."

She thought of the baby, of Judith's eyes in that pale green face, and sighed. "So it really can happen."

"Yes."

"But not for me, not for us." *Why did that hurt so much?*

"My miri, we have only been together for a few weeks. Does it always happen immediately on your planet?"

"No, of course not." She buried her head in his chest, remembering the sorrow that had swept over her when she realized that she wasn't pregnant. For once, she was actually envious of Judith. Was this longing what had originally led her sister to decide to have a baby, even without a husband? Had she been happy to have another one? Remembering the way Judith had doted on Charlie, she suspected that she had been overjoyed.

"What do we do now?"

"I need to find out what happened." He frowned. "Devoji mentioned trouble with the Dhalecs. I need to know why they are here and if they were responsible for his death."

"And if they were?"

"Then by Granthar's Hammer, he will be avenged."

Her heart lurched. "Cestov, please—"

"Daddy!" Charlie's mournful sob echoed down the hall.

"I'll go to him," he said, lifting her quickly to her feet.

"You have to tell him," she said softly.

"I know."

. . .

Cestov opened the door to find Charlie sobbing into a small stuffed animal.

"Do not cry, Charlie."

"Daddy!" The woebegone little face looked up, then he launched himself at Cestov.

He caught him easily as the small arms tightened around his neck once more. His heart ached as he wrapped a protective tail around the boy's back, wishing he could spare him pain.

"I thought you was gone again, Daddy," he said indignantly.

"No, Charlie, I'm not going to leave you. But I have to talk to you."

A dirty thumb crept into the boy's mouth.

"Charlie, I'm sorry but I'm not really your daddy. Your real daddy was my brother. We just look alike."

"Daddy..." Charlie insisted, scowling.

"No, I'm your uncle. But that is somewhat like a daddy too."

"Daddy too?" When Cestov nodded, a smile appeared on the little boy's face for the first time and he held up his hand, counting on his fingers. "Daddy one. Daddy two."

The word settled inside of him, filling his heart. "Yes, Charlie, I will be your Daddy two. Shall we go see your Aunt Mariah now?"

Charlie looked thoughtful, then held up his fingers again. "Mama two."

His chest ached. He suspected that Mariah would be thrilled. "Yes, Charlie, Mama two."

The little boy squirmed to be let down, then raced out into the hallway yelling, "Mama two, Mama two!"

A startled Mariah appeared in the bedroom doorway, then knelt to gather Charlie in her arms as he flung himself at her, still chanting "Mama two." Her eyes filled with tears again and he suspected that his own were not completely dry. Clearing his throat, he went to join them, gathering his family in his arms. They clung together until he forced himself to let go.

He helped Mariah to her feet, Charlie still wrapped in his arms, and forced himself to focus on practical matters.

"I need to contact the *Wanderer* and let them know what has happened."

"Are you going to bring her closer?"

"I do not think so. Not yet. I want to find out more about what is happening here. I'd like to talk to Devoji's brother. But I think I will ask Maldost to join us."

"I'm hungry," Charlie announced, and a surge of panic shot through him. The child must be fed, but how?

He gave Mariah a helpless look and saw that she looked just as uncertain.

"What do you usually eat, Charlie?" she asked.

He gave her a speculative look, then said, "Cookies."

From the way Mariah laughed, he suspected that the boy had asked for some kind of treat. He resolved to find out about these cookies as soon as possible.

"Why don't we go see what Devoji thinks about that?" Mariah said firmly.

They found the Granican in a spacious room obviously devoted to cooking, although he did not see any of the machines with which he was familiar. Mariah looked almost as befuddled.

"Is that a wood-burning stove?" she asked.

"No, it burns robeda dung," Devoji said.

"And my sister cooked on that?"

"Yes. She was an excellent cook."

"Well, I can assure you I'm not."

"Charlie says that he is hungry," he announced, determined to provide for the child's needs.

Devoji laughed. "He always says that. But perhaps he could have a snack now?" She raised her eyebrows at Mariah.

"Uh, sure?"

"Mistress Judith didn't like for him to spoil his dinner."

He saw Mariah's hand clench, but she gave a determined smile. "Yes, I remember she was always pretty strict about that. But I think we could all use a little something. And maybe a cup of tea?"

"Certainly." Devoji moved over to the "stove" with an odd-shaped container.

"Devoji, did my brother have an office?" he asked.

"Yes, it's through there." She nodded at a rear door. "Go past the pantry and washroom. It's the last door before the barn."

"Thank you. I would like to speak to your brother when he arrives."

"Of course. He usually comes in from the barn anyway, so you may see him before I do."

He looked at Charlie, still hesitant to leave before the child had been fed, but Mariah shooed him away. "Go ahead. See what you can find out."

When he entered his brother's office, his own fists clenched. A comfortable room with a big desk and a couple of worn, overstuffed chairs in front of a small fireplace, it was exactly what he would have expected from his brother. Unlike the sparse neatness of the rest of the house, the desk was stacked with papers and the shelves surrounding the fireplace overflowing with miscellaneous objects. Ever since they were small, Bratan had enjoyed collecting items from their travels, always complaining that he needed more space. Perhaps that had been another indication that he wasn't satisfied with the traveling life.

He wandered over to the shelves, noticing a fossilized leaf

and a small globe, before his breath caught as he recognized the familiar wooden case. The sextant. The ancient navigation device had been in their family for generations. He'd never even realized that Bratan had taken it with him.

"I'm so sorry for not listening, my brother. And now I'll never have the chance to tell you."

He stood with his head bowed for a long minute, before carefully replacing the instrument case and turning to the desk.

WHEN A NOISE IN THE CORRIDOR MADE HIM LOOK UP SOME time later, he was scowling at yet another promissory note from someone who owed Bratan for the sale of a robeda. His brother never changed—always more concerned about others than himself. Still, despite his rampant generosity, the ranch was turning a profit. Not a large one perhaps, but he did not appear to be in financial difficulty.

He looked up to find an older Granican male staring at him. He had fluffy navy hair instead of lavender, but he was clearly Devoji's brother.

"Bratan," the male whispered.

"No. I'm Cestov, his brother."

"Ah, good. For a minute there, I thought I was seeing ghosts." The male gave him a relieved smile. "I'm Devorat. Are you here because you received my message?"

"No. I found a record on Trevelor that led me here." He decided not to mention the information in the record. "My mate is with me. She is Judith's sister."

"Really? Funny how that works, isn't it?" Devorat came further into the room and flung himself down in one of the large chairs in front of the fireplace. "Have you heard about what happened?"

"Your sister said that there was a wagon accident?"

"Yes." Devorat looked at him, eyes assessing. "But she doesn't believe that and neither do I."

"Nor I. I understand he had his mate with him— he would never have taken any chances with her safety."

"No," Devorat agreed. "Never saw a more devoted male. But the marshal tried to convince us that it was because of her that he had been in a hurry. Because she had been ailing."

Despite his immediate instinct to deny it, he forced himself to think. If Mariah was ill, in need of medical assistance, would he have taken the risk?

"Perhaps," he said slowly. "But he was skilled with every type of vehicle. I do not believe that he would misjudge his skills that much."

"Yeah, that's what we thought too, but the marshal wouldn't listen." The male sat up, his face serious. "Something's not right and hasn't been since those Dhalecs showed up."

"What do they want here? They're usually mercenaries and this does not seem like the type of place that has a war brewing."

"I wish I knew." Devorat hesitated. "But I know they've been buying up land. That's why they keep demanding the ownership papers. Said if Bratan died without a will, they have first right of purchase."

"I will never sell my brother's property to them," he growled, but then he felt the weight of his words settle over him. If he could not sell this land, this ranch, what was he going to do with it? His feet felt heavy, as if he were suddenly tied in place. This wasn't what he wanted—it had never been what he wanted. But how could he abandon the place for which his brother had given his life?

## CHAPTER TWENTY

Mariah watched as Devoji bustled efficiently around the kitchen, even as she cast a rather appalled glance at the equipment. A wood-burning—make that *dung-burning*—stove? Hand-pumped water at the sink? She had traveled an unknown distance on a spaceship only to wind up on the frontier.

"When I was on Cestov's ship," she said tentatively, "He had some fancy machines to produce food."

Devoji laughed. "I'm sure he does."

"But not here?"

"No." The girl shrugged as she reached into the oven and pulled out a pie. A mouth-watering fragrance filled the room. "The machines are expensive, the supplies for them more so, and the technology required to run them doesn't mix well with our conditions."

"I suppose that makes sense."

Devoji put a soft hand on her shoulder. "It was hard for Mistress Judith at first, but she learned. You will too."

"Oh, but we're not staying."

Devoji frowned at her before turning away to cut a small slice of the pie for Charlie, carefully cutting it into small pieces and testing the temperature before she gave it to him. Oh lord, Mariah thought as she watched her. Would she have remembered to do any of those things?

Once Charlie was engrossed in his pie, Devoji sat down beside her.

"You're not staying?"

"I don't think so." She shrugged helplessly. "This is not the life we envisioned, either of us."

"But what about the children?" The girl looked from Charlie, happily smearing pie over half his face to Claire, asleep in her small cradle. "This is the only home they've ever known."

"Cestov said that he would get a bigger ship," she said.

"A ship?" Devoji looked horrified. "You can't bring children up on a spaceship. They need a place to run, to explore."

"Cestov said he and his brother were raised that way."

"And Master Bratan hated it. I heard him tell Mistress Judith many times how lucky their children were to be raised in a place where they would wake up every day to see the same sky, to fall asleep beneath the same stars every night."

Exactly what she had never wanted to do. Mariah tried her best to hide her dismay, but she must not have done a very good job because Devoji patted her hand.

"It gets easier over time," she said softly. "You just became the mother of two today."

"Mama two," Charlie crowed and they both laughed, but she could feel the underlying panic. How could she do this?

"I'm assuming you would like me to cook dinner?" Devoji said briskly.

"Oh, yes, please. That is—what did you usually do?"

"Whatever Mistress Judith wanted." The girl grinned as she went to the counter and began pulling out supplies.

"Although, I practically had to beg her to let me do anything, especially at first."

Yes, she could just imagine Judith having a hard time letting go of what she thought of as her responsibilities. "Had you been with her long?"

"About eight months. Master Bratan asked my brother to find someone to help her around the house when they realized she was pregnant. That one can be quite a handful," she said nodding at Charlie, who now had pie smeared everywhere including his hair.

"Was she happy? About the baby, I mean?"

"So happy she looked like there was a light glowing inside her. They didn't think it would happen." Devoji shot her a glance as she started peeling some type of vegetable. "Master Bratan seemed convinced that he could only have a child with a Cire female."

"Cestov thought the same thing, but we met another Cire on Trevelor with a human mate and a child."

The look that the girl aimed at her midsection was a little too obvious and Mariah forced herself to smile.

"No, I'm not pregnant."

Sorrow welled up again, even though she knew it was foolish. She had just acquired two children after all. As if in response to her thoughts, Claire began to fuss. Mariah picked her up, her heart aching again when Claire gave her a wide toothless smile and wrapped her tail around her arm.

"Would you like to feed her?" Devoji asked.

"Oh, yes."

The girl handed her a bottle. At least Mariah had given Charlie a bottle enough times to be familiar with this process and she cuddled Claire close as she fed her.

"She must know," Devoji said thoughtfully.

"Know what?"

"Who you are. I had a terrible time getting her to take a bottle at first. I finally started wrapping her in Judith's clothing and that seemed to help. She still won't take one from my mother."

She looked down at the baby sucking so contentedly on her bottle, her tiny tail wrapped around Mariah's wrist and a little bit of her worry eased. Maybe she could do this after all. She settled back in the chair and smiled at Devoji.

"You said you have a big family?"

The girl laughed and began telling her stories about her family as she moved quickly around the kitchen. When Charlie finally announced that he was done, she placed him in the sink and washed him thoroughly despite his protests, then wrapped him in a towel and brought him over to sit with Mariah by the fire.

"Sing for me, Mama two," he demanded.

Claire had finished her bottle, so Mariah cradled her in one arm and Charlie in the other and sang to them. Charlie clapped when she started "Puff the Magic Dragon" and tried to accompany her. How many times had she sung that to him before he was taken? And Judith must have continued to do the same thing. She found the thought unexpectedly comforting and by the time Cestov appeared, accompanied by a Granican male, she had found a measure of peace.

His eyes traveled over her holding the two children and she saw the same realization in his eyes. Judith and Bratan were gone, but part of their family still remained.

Devorat agreed to join them for the meal, but just as they sat down, Maldost appeared.

"Sorry, I couldn't get here sooner. That damned xuth wouldn't—"

He stopped in mid-sentence, staring at Devoji. She stared back at him just as intently and Mariah heard Devorat growl.

Oh, no. The last thing they needed right now was a case of young love.

"Who is you?" Charlie asked, his eyes wide. "You look like Pooh."

"Pooh?" Maldost asked, finally tearing his eyes away from Devoji.

Mariah choked back a laugh. "It's his stuffed animal. Do you still have that, Charlie?"

"I show you," he said immediately and started to climb down.

Cestov hauled him back up into his lap. "After dinner."

"Is Pooh staying?"

"His name is Maldost, Charlie," she said. "And yes, he's staying. Please sit down, Maldost. Unless you aren't hungry?"

As far as she could tell, he was always hungry, but he shook his head, his gaze going back to Devoji. "No, I'm not hungry, but I'll join you anyway."

Oh, this was even worse than she thought. She cast a desperate glance at Cestov, but he only smiled and shook his head.

Not until much later that night did she get a chance to be alone with Cestov. The house was quiet, but it no longer had the uneasy stillness that had greeted them on their arrival. Maldost had bedded down in Charlie's room, to Charlie's great delight. Maldost had been appropriately horrified when confronted with the bedraggled stuffed bear but he managed to smile at her little boy.

She hadn't been able to bear the thought of sleeping in Judith's room and instead, she and Cestov were on a pile of blankets in front of the fireplace in the main room. He was curled protectively around her, his tail wrapped firmly around her waist, but she knew that neither one of them were sleeping.

"I heard Devorat say that he would bring more men in the morning?"

He sighed. "Yes. I asked him to bring back the men who worked for Bratan."

She twisted around to face him. "It sounds like you plan to take over running the ranch. Do you want to stay?"

"No," he said slowly. "But I wonder if it is the right thing to do. For the children."

He looked so worried that her heart ached. She reached up to stroke his face.

"I know you didn't ask for this. If it is too much of a burden..."

"A burden? My miri, it is an honor to care for them. To have two children when I never expected to have any?" He shook his head. "I cannot deny that it is a shock, but a joyous one."

"I guess it's just as well that I wasn't pregnant."

"Never say that. Perhaps the timing would not have been ideal, but I would have done everything in my power to make it as easy as possible."

Her eyes filled with tears once more. "Cestov, I love you. I can't believe I was lucky enough to find you."

"And I you. I love you too, Mariah."

His mouth descended over hers in a kiss that went from tender to passionate as his spicy scent enveloped her. She could feel the solid ridge of his erection against her stomach and her empty pussy ached. Their time together earlier seemed much too long ago. His tail curved up under her nightshirt to tease her nipples and she moaned, trying to muffle the noise against his chest.

"I want you, my miri," he whispered, his warm breath teasing her ear and making her shiver in anticipation.

"Here?" Enough common sense penetrated her arousal for her to glance nervously around the big room.

"Yes. You just told me that you loved me and that deserves a celebration." His tongue flicked across her ear and she shivered again. "But you must be very quiet."

"Then maybe I need something to occupy my mouth." She lifted his tail higher until she could lick the wide tip. Mmm, he tasted as good here as he did everywhere else and the nubs covering his tail rubbed erotically against her tongue. She gave an experimental suck and felt him shudder.

He growled as his head fell back. "Mariah, what are you doing?"

"Being quiet." She smiled up at him and saw the hunger in his eyes.

"Then I suppose I must find something to occupy my mouth as well."

Her shirt disappeared as his head descended to her neck, kissing and nipping his way down, leaving a trail of fire behind. When he reached her breasts, he teased her nipples, just brushing them with that marvelous nubbed tongue, but always lightly, so lightly that she growled in frustration and scraped her teeth over his tail. His whole body shook and then he teased no longer. He pulled her nipple into his mouth, sucking until it was swollen and aching before moving to the other one. His hand was equally busy, parting her folds to thrust inside her with one thick digit, setting a demanding pace as his thumb worked her clit, driving her higher until she cried out his name, her voice muffled by the thick tail still filling her mouth.

Her body had not stopped trembling when she felt him at her entrance. Normally, he took her slowly, giving her time to adjust to the shock of his size, but not tonight. Tonight he entered her hard and fast, thrusting into her in a wild, erotic rhythm as she hung on to him, trying to meet his strokes as he yanked her hips higher and tighter, pounding into her as if he could never get enough, as she felt him shudder and fill her with his seed, his cock swelling in that final overwhelming stretch as he knotted deep inside and sent her flying into another explosive climax.

She clung to him, their bodies locked together, his scent surrounding her, and felt herself relax for the first time since they had arrived at the ranch. No matter what else happened, they were together. They could deal with everything else.

## CHAPTER TWENTY-ONE

"I think I need to go to town," Cestov said the next morning while they were eating breakfast. He had awoken before dawn and had spent the time until Mariah opened her eyes making plans.

Mariah's glance flew to him from where she was feeding Claire. "No, please. Can't it wait?"

"I would like to see this marshal and to hear for myself what he has to say."

"But... but what if something happens to you?" she whispered, shooting a glance at Charlie.

His son was seated on Maldost's lap, patting his fur and telling him about a hundred-acre wood. Maldost looked bemused but attentive, although Cestov saw his eyes stray to Devoji with great frequency.

"There is no reason for anything to happen," he said reassuringly. "I'm a stranger here. No one is interested in me."

"Not until you go asking questions," she muttered. "And what about the ship? And the slonga? You know Lilat's going to be very upset that we're not there."

"If we're going to be here for a while," Maldost said hopefully, "why don't we bring them here as well? Lots of land and fresh air. It would be perfect."

He had to admit it was a good idea, and he had missed seeing Lilat's little pink face looking for him this morning.

"Very well," he agreed. "This morning I will arrange for them to be brought here. I'll talk to the rest of the crew too and see what they want to do while we are here."

He couldn't quite bring himself to start making arrangements to dispose of the *Wanderer*. This ranch had been his brother's dream, not his, and it still felt like a too-tight pair of shoes. He had seen the edge of panic in Mariah's eyes as well and knew she was feeling the same way. But she loves you, he reminded himself. Everything else can be resolved.

"Daddy two, where you going?" Charlie asked suspiciously when he stood up.

"To visit my ship. I'll be back soon."

"I wants to come," he said immediately.

He looked at Mariah and she shrugged. "If you're just going to the ship and back, why not take him? I'll stay here with Devoji and Claire."

He did not want to leave her but perhaps it was for the best. He knew she was tired. Despite the passion of their lovemaking, he had woken during the night to the sound of her sobs. All he could do was hold her as she cried, his heart aching with her pain as well as his own.

"Maldost, you will remain. Stay alert."

"Yes, boss," Maldost replied, looking at Devoji who was concentrating a little too intently on scrubbing a pot.

"I want you to patrol outside the house," he said firmly, ignoring Maldost's muffled protest. "The other men will be arriving for work soon, but I want you to keep an eye out for any Dhalecs."

Maldost sobered, his ears going back. "I will. I won't let anything happen."

"I know you won't." Charlie was tugging at his knee, so he swung him up on his shoulder to a squeal of delight. "We won't be gone long."

He bent down to kiss Mariah, his heart already protesting their separation. "Do not worry, my miri."

"I'll be fine," she said bravely, although he suspected untruthfully. "Hurry back."

ON BOARD THE *WANDERER*, CHARLIE WAS AS ENTHRALLED by the slonga as they were by him. Lilat's brothers joined him in racing around the cargo hold while Tajka watched them with motherly patience. Lilat was more concerned about Cestov, exploring his face and neck with her trunk and mewling anxiously.

He asked the rest of the crew to join him on the catwalk overlooking the hold so that he could talk to them and keep his eye on his son at the same time.

"What is the situation, Captain?" Plovac asked quietly.

"It appears that we will be here for some time." He could not quite bring himself to say forever. "I need to investigate what happened to my brother."

"Debt of honor." Servisa nodded approvingly.

"Yes, exactly." He looked at the other two. Whovian was watching Charlie and the slonga play with an expression of such pain on his face that it made Cestov hurt for him, but now was not the time to ask. "I do not know how long it will take."

He filled them in on the information he had so far.

"I can stay in town," Servisa said. "Keep my eyes and ears open."

"That would be helpful. Thank you."

"If you need help at this ranch, I think I would like to spend some time planetside," Plovac said.

"I would welcome the assistance." He turned to the medic. "What of you?"

Whovian jumped and finally dragged his eyes away from Charlie. "I believe that I should remain on the *Wanderer*. You would not want to leave it unguarded."

"Perhaps not. Very well."

Plovac helped Cestov load the slonga into the wagon. Charlie was almost speechless with excitement at the thought that they would be coming out to the ranch and Cestov had to stop him from diving into the back of the wagon so that he could ride with them.

"You can see them again when we get home," he promised. *Home.* The word still felt odd in his mouth.

Back at the ranch, Maldost assured him that all had been quiet and helped set up an area in the big barn for Tajka and her calves. A high arched roof and a soft breeze blowing through the open doors at either end kept the space cool and comfortable against the increasing warmth of the day. Tajka settled into her new home with a contented sigh, but Lilat wrapped her trunk around his leg and refused to enter.

"Very well, little one," he laughed. "I'm sure Mariah would like to see you anyway."

He lifted Charlie out of the pen over his protests, and they all headed back into the house.

"Did you see Devorat on your way in?" Maldost asked. "The way he handles a xuth is incredible. It only takes a few of them to manage a whole herd of robedas."

He could hear the longing in the Afbera's voice. "Would you like to give it a try?"

"Can I?"

"I don't see why not. Plovac, do you mind staying here at the house to keep an eye on things this afternoon?"

"Of course not. But are you leaving?" Plovac asked.

"I need to go into town," he said.

"I wanna go," Charlie demanded.

"Not this afternoon, little one." The boy's lip quivered, and he almost gave in before he remembered that it might not be safe. "Besides, don't you want to stay and play with the slonga?"

"I guess."

"I'll be back before you know it," he promised.

After a quick lunch, he drove into town. He hated to leave Mariah again, especially when he could see the worry in her eyes, but his honor and his love for his brother demanded that he investigate further.

At first glance, Selo didn't seem any different than on the previous day, but now that he was aware that there might be trouble, he caught the signs he had not noticed before. More than one person stopped in their tracks at the sight of him, then hastily moved away, averting their eyes. He saw four more of the Dhalecs although again, they weren't doing anything wrong, despite their threatening appearance.

The marshal's office had a sign stating that he would return in an hour, so he wandered down the main street. The place seemed prosperous enough in a small-town way. Several small restaurants, a couple of drinking places, and a small clinic were intermixed with several stores, and a few official-looking buildings. The largest store was located in the center of town and he decided to take a look around.

As he entered, the varied scents washed over him and he had a sudden vivid memory of when he was small and he and Bratan had visited their father's store on Ciresia. It had been much larger and grander of course, but something about this place felt familiar. A large central space held a wide variety of items, while small areas lining the sides were dedicated to specific products.

"How can I help you, sir?"

A stout little Granican with thinning pale blue hair came hurrying out of the back. He stopped dead in his tracks at the sight of Cestov.

"Bratan?" he whispered, his face paling.

"No. He is—was—my brother. Did you know him?"

"Umm, no. No," he added more firmly. "Just seen him around, that's all."

Cestov wasn't sure he believed him, but he nodded amiably. "Nice place you have here."

The little man beamed. "I'm sure you don't think it's much but it's one of the finest in this part of Granica."

"Why would I think that?"

"Oh, because of all the places you've been..." He ground to a stop.

"How do you know where I've been?"

The shopkeeper cast a wild look around, as if waiting for someone else to appear and answer the question, then finally stepped closer.

"Please, Cestov—"

"I never told you my name."

"No. Bratan told me," the male admitted. "But he tried to help us and look what happened." He lowered his voice with another look around. "You should leave here. Leave now before it's too late and—"

"Radna. What are you up to today?" A Dhalec strode through the door, showing an impressive array of teeth between his tusks in what apparently passed for a smile. "Has my order come in?"

Radna jumped and left Cestov's side to hurry over to his

new customer, wringing his hands. "No. I'm sorry, Basno. I put a rush on it, but you know how the shipping is from Luka to here. I'm very sorry but there's only so much I can do—"

Basno waved a hand, his beady eyes fixing on Cestov. "And who is this? A new resident in our town?"

"I'm sure he's just passing through," Radna said quickly.

"No. Actually, I'm thinking of staying. My brother has a ranch here."

Did the Dhalec react? He wasn't quite sure, but his instincts were shouting at him.

"Granica can be a tough place to build a ranch," Basno drawled, then bared his teeth in that pointed grin. "Not everyone is cut out for it."

"I do not give up easily." He bared his own teeth before turning back to the merchant. "Nice to meet you, Radna. I'm sure I'll be seeing you again."

The little shopkeeper lost himself in a confused mumble as his gaze darted between him and the Dhalec. Cestov nodded and left, turning the visit over in his mind. Was Radna so uneasy simply because of the Dhalec? Had he been trying to warn him or to warn him away?

His visit to the marshal's office left him with even more questions. Marshal Zakon was a large Granican with a thick head of navy hair and an oversized stomach that he rubbed complacently as he leaned back in his chair.

"Boy was speeding."

"My brother was skilled in driving all types of vehicles. And he would never have taken risks with his mate's safety."

For the briefest instant, the male's composure cracked. "Shame about that. She was a nice little thing. And leaving those kids behind." He shook his head. "Good thing you came to get 'em and take 'em away from here."

"Actually, I'm thinking of staying."

"Staying?" Zakon sat upright. "Not sure that's a good idea."

"Why not?" He arched a brow ridge.

"Well, those kids. Should get them away from all the bad memories."

"Perhaps. In the meantime, I would like to see the accident report."

"Umm, it's already been archived."

"Then retrieve it." He leaned down over the marshal and saw sweat appear on his brow.

"Might take some time."

"As I said, I'm not going anywhere. And I will be back." With a frustrated growl, he turned and left.

His third visit was to the town bank. Unlike the first two interviews, the bank manager, Macduk, seemed completely unfazed by the sight of him. When Cestov explained who he was, he nodded sympathetically.

"Very sad circumstances. Very sad, indeed. I suppose you're interested in selling the ranch?"

"Not at all," he said firmly, anticipating resistance, but Macduk only nodded.

"Your decision, of course. Now I assume you want to take ownership of the ranch accounts?"

The rest of their business was conducted quickly and amicably, Macduk clasping his hand warmly when they were finished.

"If you have any questions, don't hesitate to call on me."

"I won't. Thank you."

As he headed for his wagon, he spotted Servisa sitting outside one of the restaurants but didn't acknowledge him. They had agreed that it might be better if no one suspected their connection. Frustration gnawed at him as he climbed into his vehicle, but the knowledge that Mariah and the children were waiting for him made him increase his speed. Time to go home.

# CHAPTER TWENTY-TWO

Mariah heaved a frustrated sigh as she took her attempt at a pie out of the oven. The edges were burnt, and the middle sagged in a suspicious way. Devoji's pie was a vision of golden perfection.

"Don't worry, Mariah," Devoji said. "Mistress Judith had to learn as well."

"Did she ever make one that looked this bad?"

"Well, no."

They both laughed and Devoji took the misshapen pie and put it on a shelf next to the sink. "I will have my brother add it to the food for the robedas."

"I hope they have strong stomachs," she said doubtfully.

"They will eat anything," Devoji assured her, then flushed. "I mean..."

"It's all right. I know what you mean. You know, if you told Maldost that you baked it, I'm sure he wouldn't hesitate to eat it."

The girl's flush deepened. "He is a kind male."

"Yes, he is." Abandoning her teasing, she paced restlessly to the kitchen door. "I wonder how much longer it'll be until Cestov returns. He's been gone so long."

"Probably not until late afternoon," Devoji said calmly, but Mariah could see a reflection of her own worry in the girl's eyes.

"I need something to do—and cooking is apparently not my strength."

Claire chose that moment to start fussing and Devoji laughed again. "I think someone wants your attention."

"Hi, sweetheart. Did you just wake up?"

She picked up the baby and sang to her softly while Devoji prepared her bottle.

"Mistress Judith used to do that," the girl said as she handed it to her.

"What's that?"

"Sing to her. To both of them. She told Charlie she used to sing to you when you were little."

Unexpected tears filled her eyes. How many years had it been since she'd thought about that? But she remembered Judith singing to her, remembered how that had started her own love of music. Would her sister still have done it if she'd known it would set her on such a different path than she had envisioned for her life? Yes, she decided, as she looked down at Claire, studying her intently while she sucked. Judith would still have wanted her to be happy.

When Claire finished, Mariah lifted her to her shoulder as she wandered around the room. "Do you have a carrier for her? I thought maybe I would go sweep the courtyard."

"I can do that. I'm sorry I haven't been taking—"

"Devoji, stop. I'm not criticizing you. You've done a wonderful job of looking after the children and taking care of the ranch. I can never thank you enough." She flashed the girl a watery smile. "I just thought the tiles might be safer from my efforts than the food."

"Are you sure?"

"Yes, of course. You can even send Charlie out once he wakes up from his nap."

The last time she had checked, he was sprawled on his bed, one arm stretched over Lilat, who had curled up next to him. The slonga had never had an accident on the ship and she only hoped that meant she was house-trained as well.

A short time later, she had Claire tied securely to her front while she started on the courtyard. The sky overhead was a brilliant blue that shaded into lavender but the way the house was oriented cast enough shade to make the afternoon only pleasantly warm. Today, all of the shutters were open, and the oppressive silence had vanished. It was still a lot more rustic than she was used to, but she was beginning to believe that Judith had been happy here. Maybe she could be as well.

She had made considerable progress before a noise made her look up. Plovac had set up a watchpoint on the flat roof of the house and he called down to her now.

"It's the captain, Mistress Mariah."

Thank god. Her heart thudded with relief and she smiled down at Claire. "That's your daddy. He's coming home."

Cestov didn't go straight to the barn but brought the wagon to a halt right outside the gate. Her pulse increased at the sight of her big warrior striding towards her.

"My miri, I've missed you," he said as he pulled her into his arms and his tail wrapped around her waist. His scent filled her nostrils and she felt the tension leave her body. He was home.

"I missed you too."

He kissed her until she melted against him and Claire let out a squeak.

"Sorry, little one," he said apologetically. "May I hold her?"

"Of course."

She unwrapped the baby and handed her over, showing him how to support her, but his tail had already curved behind her head. Claire's own miniature version wrapped around his wrist.

"It is so strange to see your eyes in her face," he murmured.

"My sister's eyes. Do you see your brother in her?"

"Perhaps. Her features are so small and delicate it's hard to be sure." He looked up and smiled at her. "I see you have been getting busy. And dirty."

She laughed as he flicked a speck of dirt off her nose. "Apparently, I'm no use in the kitchen, but I wield a mean broom. What do you think?"

"It looks much better," he agreed as he looked around, then frowned at the sundial with the pedestal on its side. "Take Claire for a moment, please."

Once he handed over the baby, he stood the pedestal upright and brushed off the dial. "It will have to be calibrated to this place," he said, his voice odd.

"Cestov, is something wrong?"

"The sundial. They are based on the movement of the sun on a particular planet. Bratan carried one around on the ship for years, but of course, there isn't a single sun in space. Do you remember what Devoji said? That the children would wake up knowing that they would see the same sky every day? He must have been so happy to be able to place this here. For his family."

"Our family," she said softly as she came to stand next to him with Claire in her arms.

His tail wrapped around them both. "Our family."

After dinner that night, everyone gathered in the big living room. To her delight, Cestov had brought the dobron from the ship. She was a long way from being an expert, but she'd already learned enough to accompany herself on a few songs. Devoji sat to one side of the fireplace and blushed when Maldost asked to sit next to her, but Mariah noticed that she didn't refuse. Despite the heat of the day, the nights cooled off enough to make the fire enjoyable, although she still wasn't sure how she felt about the fact that they were burning dung. At least it only had a faint leafy tang when it burned.

Fresh from his bath, Charlie curled up on Cestov's lap. Cestov cradled Claire carefully in his other arm while the three of them listened to her sing, but the little boy only lasted through a few songs. Devoji accompanied her as she carried him to bed and drew her aside once they left his room.

"While you were outside this afternoon, I made some changes. I hope you will approve."

"Changes?"

"Yes, come and see."

The girl led her to the main bedroom and Mariah looked around in amazement. The room no longer bore the stamp of Judith's personality. Her pillows and curtains were gone, replaced by simple white linens. The furniture had been rearranged so that the bed overlooked the small rear courtyard and a bowl of flowers filled the room with a sweet scent.

"You shouldn't be sleeping on the floor. I know it was hard for you to be in here, so I wanted to give you a fresh start. I hope I did the right thing."

For a moment, she wanted to protest, then she nodded slowly. The room did feel different, but she hadn't lost the memory of her sister.

"Yes, Devoji. Thank you." She smiled tremulously. "A bed would definitely be an improvement."

When she led Cestov down the hallway later that night, he obviously approved as well.

"I approve, my miri. That is—if you are sure?"

"Yes. I don't need to keep her room as a shrine to remember her by."

"Then I very much intend to put that bed to use," he said, advancing on her with a gleam in his eyes that made her nipples peak and her pussy dampen.

"Oh?" she asked innocently. "What did you have in mind?"

"I noticed that this bed is a perfect height."

"A perfect height for what?"

"For this."

Her shirt disappeared with a quick yank, then he ripped her pants away with effortless strength.

"Cestov, I don't have that many clothes. *You* have to stop tearing them off me."

"They are in my way." His eyes gleamed. "And I much prefer you this way, exposed to my view."

"I like you naked too, but you're still clothed—"

His clothes disappeared in a flash and he stalked closer, his thick, heavy shaft reaching for her. Her mouth went dry even as the slickness between her thighs increased. How did she ever manage to take that massive cock? She bent down, licking the thick nubbed length, and felt him shudder, but he pulled her away.

"As I was saying, this bed is the perfect height."

He picked her up and placed her upper body across it face down, leaving her legs to dangle.

"It's too tall," she said breathlessly.

"Not for me. Your sweet little cunt is perfectly placed." He nudged the thick head of his cock against her entrance as he spoke, groaning his appreciation at the slick heat waiting for him. "You are very wet, my miri."

"You seem to have that effect on... Oh god," she cried as he slid into her slowly and inexorably, the stretch almost too much as he filled her unprepared body, but the nubs sliding across her sensitive flesh turned the stretching burn to an aching pleasure.

He stroked his hands down her back, gentling her, as he waited for her body to adjust. His big hands covered her buttocks, then spread them apart in order to tease the sensitive crevice. Wet heat teased her bottom hole and she realized that his tail was circling the delicate flesh.

"Can you take more, my miri?" he asked, his voice dark and seductive. "Do you want me filling all of you?"

She hesitated and he moved his hips, just a little but enough to send a wave of desire washing over her. Her clit throbbed and her pussy tightened around him.

"Your body seems to approve."

He adjusted his position again and she felt him stroke lightly—too lightly—across her swollen clit. She arched back into that frustrating touch and his tail breached the tight ring. *Oh god.* She shivered and he stroked her back again.

"Relax, Mariah. Or do you want me to stop?"

No. She wanted more of this tantalizing stretch, of this overwhelming fullness. More of him.

"No," she gasped.

"Good girl." He swept over her clit again, harder this time, and his tail slid in another inch. Sparks of fire shot through her body and she shivered again. The movement caused her nipples to rub against the coverlet, adding to the desire mounting within her.

"Please, Cestov."

He started to pull out, leaving a trail of fire behind but he paused halfway, then thrust back in with a quick hard jerk that had her seeing stars. More, she wanted more, and when he paused again, she tried to push back against him. Her response seemed to unleash all of his restraint. He stroked into her hard and fast, his hand pressing against her clit so that each thrust sent a wave of pleasure shooting through her. His tail moved deeper, the burn increasing but only adding to the fiery pleasure that was creeping over her. Her nipples ached, her clit throbbed, her pussy tightened, and her vision sheeted white as her climax roared over her in wave after wave of pleasure. She heard him cry out her name, felt him thrust impossibly deeper as his cock swelled and knotted, the pressure sending her straight into another long rolling climax before he collapsed down over her.

"Mmm, you were right," she whispered when she finally regained enough strength to speak.

"About what?" He sounded just as tired and satisfied.

"This bed is the perfect height."

He laughed, the vibration rolling through their interlocked bodies so that they both moaned.

"Only because I have the perfect mate," he whispered.

A lump formed in her throat and she reached for his hand, clasping it in demonstration of the feelings she didn't have the words to say.

## CHAPTER TWENTY-THREE

A small foot digging into his ribs awoke Cestov the next morning. He grunted and opened his eyes to find Charlie standing over him. The sight of his son—the son he had never thought to have—filled him with happiness.

"Good morning to you too," he said and pulled Charlie down next to him, gently tickling his ribs.

The boy squealed with laughter and Mariah opened sleepy eyes.

"Apparently, someone thinks it's time we were up."

"Up, up," Charlie agreed.

From down the hall, Claire cried out and Mariah laughed as she sat up. "I guess everyone thinks it's time we were up." She smothered a yawn. "Someone kept me up way too late last night."

"I'm sorry, my miri."

"Are you?" she asked, raising one of her adorable little furry brows.

Remembering her body stretched out before him, her tight

clasp around his cock and his tail, the way she had flooded him with her pleasure, he shook his head. "Not at all."

"Me neither." She dropped a quick kiss on his lips and started to climb out of the bed just as Devoji appeared in the doorway that Charlie had left open with Claire in her arms.

"I'm sorry," she said, blushing. "But I thought you might want to feed the little one?"

"Of course."

Mariah retrieved Claire and the bottle and climbed back into bed, nursing the baby while Charlie told them in complicated and somewhat unintelligible detail about his plans for the day. Listening to his son while his mate fed their daughter filled him with contentment. He still was not entirely convinced about the benefits of staying in a single location, but about this, he had no doubts.

Charlie finally ran down and after watching Mariah feed Claire, announced that he was hungry as well. Cestov fought back his immediate panic at the thought that he wasn't providing for his son and forced himself to remember that it didn't mean that Charlie was in need.

"Then let's get you to the kitchen," he said. "I'm sure Devoji has something prepared."

"Want Mama two to feed me," he said, poking the bottle with his finger.

"But you're a big boy," Mariah said gently. "Remember? Claire is just a baby."

"I guess."

Charlie's lower lip still stuck out, so Cestov lifted him up on his shoulder with a whooshing sound. To his relief, Charlie squealed happily, grabbed his head, and rode him into the kitchen without further complaint.

After breakfast, he decided he needed to get a better feel for the ranch and asked Devorat to accompany him on a ride around the property. Plovac agreed to stand watch once more while Maldost accompanied them. Charlie wasn't happy to be left behind but Mariah distracted him with the promise of making cookies.

"Or rather Devoji will make cookies with him," she said with a rueful smile as she accompanied him to the barn. "I don't seem to have the knack for pioneer cooking. I miss the machines on your ship."

"I can transfer them," he offered immediately.

"I'm tempted, but it might not be the best idea. Devoji said they don't work well here and it's hard to get supplies." She leaned against him and stroked his tail. "Are you going to be gone all day again?"

"No. Just a few hours."

Despite his reassuring words, he wasn't any happier about the separation than she was. He missed their time on the *Wanderer* where they were never more than a few rooms apart. The noose of the ranch tightened around his throat, but he did his best to ignore it.

This was his brother's legacy and it was best for the children. He would adjust.

He did find an unexpected pleasure in riding out into the morning. The gently rolling hills were lush with the low-cropped vegetation. Two of the world's moons still hung low overhead, shedding a soft light on the peaceful scene. The herds of robedas ambled around, chewing gently, while the men he had hired watched over them from their xuths. He admired the way they handled the ungainly animals. He had proven competent but nothing more and he already suspected that Maldost would rapidly surpass him. His young crew member was deep in a discussion with Devorat about the way the herds were managed, and Cestov was surprised by how much the young Afbera had already picked up. Maldost looked happy here, he thought, already at home.

They rode along the boundary line towards one of the low hills as Devorat described the different areas.

"This land isn't much use for the robedas," he said, gesturing at the increasingly rocky ground. "Not enough vegetation and they have a tendency to disappear into the canyons where they're hard to track. Dammit, there's one now."

They all turned to look as a robeda appeared amongst the rocks. The animals had a single massive horn extending from their foreheads, and this one seemed to be having an issue with her horn. She kept tossing its head back and forth as she stumbled towards them.

"What's wrong with her?" Maldost asked.

"I don't know." Devorat frowned. "Let's go see if we can head her back towards the herd."

As they neared, the animal swayed to the right, then turned in a circle before swaying to the left.

"She looks like she's drunk," Maldost said.

"Drunk? Oh, fuck." Devorat spurred his xuth closer, jumping off next to the animal that had now collapsed.

By the time they caught up with him, Devorat had already risen to his feet, shaking his head.

"We're too late. Fuck. I really thought we had eradicated that stuff."

"What's wrong?"

"You see the green foam on her mouth? She's been eating brillat seeds."

"What's brillat?"

"One of the plants that grows amongst the rocks. A small amount won't hurt the cattle but taken in large quantities, it's fatal. I don't know where she would have found so much. We went through here a year ago and burned it out."

"You can't save her?" Maldost asked, staring at the robeda.

"I'm afraid not. Once they're down, it's too late." Devorat reached for his gun. "I'm going to put her out of her misery."

Cestov expected his soft-hearted crew member to turn away, but he only nodded, his face pale and serious, and watched as Devorat quickly dispatched the dying beast.

"I want to ride up into the hills," Devorat said as he rejoined them. "To see if we can spot the patch."

Cestov nodded and they followed the Granican further into the hills. He found himself envying the ease with which both Devorat and Maldost handled their xuths over the rough terrain. As they came around a rock outcropping, Devorat came to a halt. When Cestov pulled his xuth to a stop and looked up, he understood why. A small valley lay in front of them, every inch covered in low plants in a rich green color.

"Brillat?" he asked.

"Yes," Devorat said grimly. "And it never grows like this under normal conditions. Someone planted it."

"Why would they do that? To poison our herds?"

Devorat frowned, then shook his head. "It seems unlikely. As I said, we try and keep them far from the hills. That one must have wandered off undetected, perhaps in the confusion after your brother's death."

"Does the brillat have any value?"

"Not of which I'm aware. My grandmother used to make a medicinal tea from it. It combines a numbing effect with a slight euphoria, but it is easy to drink too much and become incapacitated."

"Sounds like drinking too much ale," Maldost snorted.

Cestov shook his head. "You would have to drink a lot of ale for that to happen. This, on the other hand…"

He turned back to Devorat. "The effect of the tea—it is pleasant?"

"Why, yes. I suppose so. I've never tried it, but my grandmother spoke of a feeling of energy and excitement. But it is also quite addictive, and she decided it was too dangerous. Most Granicans know to stay away from it."

"Then you are a sensible people," he said grimly. "I am very much afraid that someone has decided that there could be a market for this off-world."

"Which would explain why the Dhalecs are here," Maldost pointed out.

"Agreed. But they are just mercenaries. Someone else is behind this, and I suspect it is someone local."

"One of us?" Devorat looked shocked. "I cannot believe that. As you said, we are a sensible people."

"Unfortunately, the promise of wealth had corrupted many a sensible male. And female." He turned to survey the expanse of green. "Does this land belong to the ranch?"

"Technically, yes, although we have never used it."

"No wonder someone was trying so hard to purchase it," he said grimly. "Will it burn?"

Devorat looked at him, then nodded. "Aye. This is the dry season."

"Is it likely to spread? To cause damage to anything else?"

"No. You can see that vegetation is sparse here in the hills." Devorat dismounted. "I approve of your idea, but you realize that someone is going to be upset."

"Good." He bared his teeth. "Then perhaps we will find out who is at the bottom of this. And who killed my brother."

He and Maldost joined Devorat and together the three of them set the brillat on fire, watching as the field of green gradually turned to ash. The sun was high overhead when the last ember died down and all that was left was a grey residue.

"We should return to the house. My mate will be worried, and I wish to let her know about this."

As they rode back down through the hills, Maldost asked, "Do you think we can expect an open attack?"

"I do not know. So far everything has been done quietly. Whoever is behind this does not want to reveal his hand. But I think perhaps it is time to bring the *Wanderer* closer. She should discourage any foolish attempts."

Devorat nodded. "A sound plan. I will also check with Father to see if more of my brothers can join us. I will keep everyone working in pairs."

"Thank you." He shot the Granican a quick glance. "Have you been pressured to sell your land?"

"No, but our property does not border on the hills. I realize now that every parcel that has been bought is connected to them in some way. I believe this is the last homestead that's still privately owned."

"And those bastards killed my brother to get their hands on it."

"I think so. I'm surprised that they didn't push harder to take possession after his death, but with Devoji staying at the ranch and no one going up in the hills, they probably assumed they had time."

"Their time has run out," he said grimly.

## CHAPTER TWENTY-FOUR

As soon as they returned to the ranch, Cestov pulled Mariah aside to explain the situation.

"Someone planted drugs? On Judith's property?" she said, outraged. "She would be so pissed—she hated drugs."

"They are not there anymore," he promised. "But we need to find out who is behind this."

"You don't think it's those ugly blue guys?"

"The Dhalecs? No, I don't. I think someone hired them, but I suspect that the true culprit is probably a Granican."

"I can't believe that. They're all so nice."

"Not all people are alike. Just like Kwaret was a good Vedeckian, perhaps there is a bad Granican. Who else would have had the knowledge of that plant and what it can do?"

"I suppose you're right," she said reluctantly. "What are you going to do now?"

"I'm going back to town. That shopkeeper tried to warn me off. I find it hard to believe that he's behind it, but I think he knows something."

"Do you think he'll talk to you?"

"I know he will," he said grimly.

"Are you sure you have to do this? If this is anything like the drug trade on Earth, it could be terribly dangerous. I couldn't stand it if anything happened to you."

Her eyes filled with tears and he pulled her close, stroking her back with his tail.

"I know it's not without risk, but I was brought up as a warrior."

"Your brother was too, and it didn't save him."

The familiar guilt made his heart ache. Would it have been different if he had been here?

"I know, but I don't think he knew what was happening or why someone was after his land. And whoever is doing this is trying to keep it quiet. That's in my favor."

She cast a nervous glance out at the quiet ranch. "What if something happens while you're gone?"

"Before I head to town, I'm going to take Plovac to the *Wanderer* and have him fly her back here. He can land on the back pasture. The sight of a fully armed spaceship should dissuade anyone from doing something stupid. I'll take the shuttle into town so I can avoid the roads. Just in case," he added.

She tried to smile at him, but it was a woeful effort.

"Do not worry, my miri. Everything will be fine."

His words didn't help, and tears started to trickle down her cheeks.

"Why's you making Mama two cry?" Charlie tugged on his leg, his little face belligerent.

"He's not making me cry, sweetheart," Mariah said quickly, wiping her tears away. "I'm just feeling a little emotional."

He scuffed his foot on the ground. "You miss Mama?"

"Yes, Charlie. Very much. And I'm sure you do too."

He nodded and buried his face in her skirts. Cestov knelt down next to him, his heart aching.

"It's okay to miss them, Charlie. But we can remember how much we loved them and how much they loved us."

Charlie nodded, then threw his arms around Cestov's neck. "Love you, Daddy two."

"And I love you, Charlie." He stood up with the boy in one arm and gathered Mariah into the other. As he held them close, he vowed he would never let anything happen to his family.

"Charlie, I'm going to bring the ship back here. Do you want to come along?"

"Are we gonna fly to the stars?" the boy asked, his eyes wide.

"Not today, son. Just back to the ranch."

"Yay!" Charlie cheered and grinned at the two of them, his little face happy again.

When they arrived at the *Wanderer*, Whovian paled at the sight of Charlie and disappeared into his lab. Cestov had Plovac show Charlie the controls while he went to find his medic.

"What's wrong, Whovian? Is it Charlie?"

"Yes and no. It's not him, but he reminds me of what I could have had."

"Yes?" he asked. He had not pried into the medic's past, but he suspected that he had found the source of his pain.

"There was a female," Whovian began. "She... cared for me but I was young and foolish, and I did not appreciate that gift as I should have. When she came to me and told me that she was with child, I did not believe her. I performed a test but perhaps I was impatient or perhaps I was careless, I do not know. I told her that it was negative and sent her away."

"What happened?"

"I left with the next ship but to my surprise, I could not forget her. Eventually, I went back." He looked up; his eyes so full of pain that Cestov's breath caught. "She died—she and my child died because there was no one with the medical knowledge to assist them. It was my fault."

"If you would rather not stay on the ranch, do you want to accompany me into town? That might be easier."

"Yes. Please. I know this is a weakness, but I need more time."

Cestov went to say a quick goodbye to Charlie, who was too awed by the prospect of flying to protest. How much he wished he could have witnessed his son's excitement in his first flight, but it was more important to find the culprit behind the brillat plants.

As soon as the ship departed, he aimed the shuttle for Selo, flying overland straight towards it rather than follow the roads. Once they landed, he headed for the main store, determined to get some information from the shopkeeper. Whovian accompanied him, studying the town with interest.

No one was in the store when he entered and Radna didn't come bustling out to meet him. Too afraid, no doubt.

"Radna," he called impatiently.

There was a faint answering moan from the back of the building. He and Whovian took off at a run. The small shopkeeper was crumpled behind a set of shelves, blood flowing from a gaping wound in his side.

"Fuck," Whovian swore as he reached for his satchel. He pulled out a syringe and administered a quick anesthetic, then began packing the wound with gauze. "I need to get him to a medical center. Does this godsforsaken town have anything like that?"

"I saw a small clinic about two blocks away from here when I was looking around."

"It will have to do."

Whovian gathered the male carefully in his arms and stood up, but Radna reached out and grabbed Cestov's sleeve.

"Macduk," he whispered. "Behind everything…"

His words trailed off as his eyes fluttered shut.

The banker? Fuck. By Granthar's Hammer, the male was going to pay. He hurried with Whovian to the clinic. People gasped as they raced by with the small male covered with blood. If they didn't already know something was wrong, they knew it now, he reflected grimly.

The clinic turned out to be a neat, well-equipped medical center but there was no medic on duty. A brisk, efficient female explained that they were trying to hire someone as she led the way into the small operating room.

"Can you assist me?" Whovian asked.

She paled but nodded resolutely.

"Good. Cestov, go find that bastard."

"You do not need me?"

"Not unless you've had medical training in the past ten minutes." He peered at the female. "Not going to faint on me, are you?"

"I am not the fainting type," she said tartly and Whovian's lips quirked before he nodded at Cestov.

"We'll be fine. Go."

He nodded and took off. Clusters of people gathered in the streets, whispering to each other and staring as he went by, but he ignored them. He stalked into the bank and headed straight for Macduk's office.

"Wait a minute!" a young Granican clerk cried. "You can't go back there."

"I'm going to see Macduk," he growled without pausing.

"But he's not there."

He stopped and turned to face the young male. The clerk stuttered and took a step back.

"Where is he?"

"I'm not sure. He said something about going to visit a ranch?"

His heart started to pound. "A ranch? Which one?"

"I don't know. Two of those big males showed up after lunch and locked themselves in with him."

"You mean the Dhalecs?"

"Yes. I heard a lot of shouting and swearing. But then they left, and he came out a little bit later and said he had to make a visit."

Fuck. A thousand horrible scenarios played through his head. "But you don't know where?"

The clerk shook his head but Cestov couldn't take the chance that it was unrelated. "Go to the medical clinic. Tell the medic there that I had to leave. I do not know when I'll be back. Got it?"

"Y-yes."

He raced back outside to find Servisa approaching him, his big red body head-and-shoulders above the Granicans who were gathering in even larger groups now.

"Captain!" Servisa called. "I think I have some news."

"Get in the shuttle and tell me on the way," he ordered.

Servisa took one look at his face and didn't argue. The two of them raced for the small vessel while his heart pounded so hard he felt sick. Maldost is there, he reminded himself. Maldost and Plovac and all the rest of the men. They would be fine. But his body didn't believe him. His hands shook as he took off, skimming across the ground with reckless speed.

"What did you find out?" he asked Servisa.

"Heard a couple of the Dhalecs talking earlier. Bitching

about the job being dull. One of them said at least they knew they were going to get paid because a banker always has access to money."

His hand clenched on the steering column. "I think he's headed for the ranch."

Servisa swore and did not protest as Cestov increased his speed, pushing the small craft to its absolute limit, praying with every fiber of his being that he was not too late.

# CHAPTER TWENTY-FIVE

After Cestov left, Mariah paced restlessly, unable to calm down, until she realized that she was making everyone else just as nervous. Charlie's normal good nature had disappeared, and he had a screaming fit when she told him they couldn't make cookies right away. By the time she got him calmed down, they were both exhausted. Even Devoji seemed unusually moody.

Determined to find some sense of calm, she gathered all of them in the living room for some music. By the time she finished the second repetition of "Hakuna Matata," Charlie was marching happily around the room and Devoji was smiling again. When she heard the bell, her heart skipped a beat but then she forced herself to relax. She knew the men were outside and they wouldn't let anyone dangerous near the house.

Leaving Devoji to look after the children, Mariah went to answer the door. An older Granican stood on the veranda. He had the thick body of a well-fed male and a cloud of white hair groomed into a modest peak. He beamed as she answered the door.

"Ah. You must be Mistress Mariah. Your mate told me so much about you."

"He did?"

"Yes, of course. I'm sorry—I forgot to introduce myself. I am Macduk, President of the Selo Bank. Your mate spoke to me about transferring his brother's accounts into his name."

Her tense shoulders relaxed. Cestov had mentioned his visit to the bank, as well as the fact that the banker had been one of the few to meet him without fear or suspicion.

"I'm sorry, but he's not here right now." She winced internally as she realized that she had told him that they were alone. "But he'll be back any minute," she added hastily.

"Good, good. Then perhaps I can come in to wait for him?"

Damn. That hadn't worked out the way she intended. Still, the manners that her sister had drilled into her had her opening the door and gesturing him inside. As she went to close the door, she saw Maldost watching from the entrance to the barn. He lifted an inquiring hand and after a brief moment, she nodded and waved.

Once inside, Macduk was full of praise for both the house and the ranch.

"I'm glad to know that you're going to keep it in the family," he said with a solemn nod. "These family ranches are the backbone of Granica."

He admired the baby and tried to make friends with Charlie, but the little boy had reverted to his earlier bad mood and merely scowled at him. Mariah and Devoji exchanged a helpless look as the older male wandered around the room, rambling on about the history of the settlement.

"Umm, would you like some tea?" she finally asked.

"Why, yes. That would be most delightful. The ritual of tea drinking is one of the high points of civilization…" And he was off on another seemingly endless lecture.

Devoji returned with the tea tray and they all gathered uncomfortably in front of the fireplace.

*At least I don't have to make polite conversation*, Mariah thought as Macduk continued to pontificate, this time about the absence of manners in the younger generation.

Claire began to fuss, and Mariah picked her up while Devoji prepared her bottle. Once the baby had been fed and returned to her cradle, she gave Macduk a fixed smile.

"It seems like my mate has been delayed. Maybe it would be best if you return to town and I'll let him know that you were here."

"Yes, yes. Perhaps that would be for the best." He picked up his cup and sipped with every evidence of enjoyment. "Aren't you going to have some of this excellent tea? A delightful blend."

If it would hurry him along... She picked up her cup and drained what was left. The tea had grown bitter from standing but she successfully suppressed her wince. Devoji also finished her cup and as soon as the young girl put it down, Mariah rose to her feet.

"Thank you for joining us. I will be sure and give Cestov your message."

"Thank you for your hospitality," he said benevolently as they walked to the door.

She had only gone a few feet when the world started to spin. She wobbled and threw her hand out and Macduk caught it, holding onto her with surprising strength.

"I'm sorry. I'm just a little dizzy."

"Perhaps you should sit down." He led her to a chair, but her vision was growing increasingly clouded. His face swam in and out of focus, but she could tell he was smiling.

"Wh-what's happening to me?"

"Just a little concoction of my mother's. She was quite the herbalist in her day, you know."

Her face felt numb and unresponsive, but it must have reflected her horror because he nodded. "Yes, that's right. She was the one who gave me the idea to sell the brillat seeds off-planet."

"What's wrong, Mama?" Charlie popped up at her elbow, his blue eyes anxious.

As much as she tried, she couldn't speak. The last thing she saw as the world went black was Macduk's hand covering Charlie's mouth.

Mariah had no idea how much time had passed when she regained consciousness, her head pounding and a bitter taste filling her mouth. Forcing her reluctant body to sit up, she scanned the room. Devoji had collapsed on the floor next to the coffee table and she could hear faint snuffling noises coming from the cradle. But where was Charlie? Both he and Macduk had disappeared. The adrenaline surging through her system gave her the strength to push herself to her feet.

"Charlie...!" she called hoarsely, even though her sinking heart did not expect an answer. Her gaze went to the front door. Macduk had to have left through there and surely, someone would have stopped him if he had Charlie with him. She staggered in that direction, her knees unsteady. Her trembling hands fought to release the catch, but she finally pushed the door open and almost fell out onto the veranda. She clutched one of the posts desperately, searching for any trace of her son.

Cestov's shuttle appeared, skidding to a halt outside the wall. Cestov leaped out almost before it stopped moving. He reached her just as her knees gave way.

"He's got him. Macduk's got Charlie."

He swore long and viciously as he lifted her carefully into his arms, then turned to yell at Servisa.

"Get Maldost and Plovac. Start questioning everyone! Someone must have seen something."

He carried her into the house, where Claire's soft snuffles had turned into full-fledged cries.

"The baby," she cried, starting to struggle against his arms.

"Sit here," he ordered as he lowered her into one of the chairs. "I'll get her."

Almost as soon as he put Claire in her arms, the baby's cries diminished, and she wrapped her tiny tail around Mariah's wrist. Thank god that bastard hadn't done anything to her.

Maldost burst through the door, his gaze going immediately to Devoji, still crumpled on the floor. He snarled, the expression on his face almost frightening, no longer the sweet oversized young male but a vicious predator. Gathering the girl up in his arms, he gently patted her face.

"Devoji, speak to me." There was no response and he gave Mariah a desperate look. "What's wrong with her?"

"We were drugged." Both Cestov and Maldost growled. "I think it'll take longer for her to come around because she's so small."

"Where's Whovian?" Maldost demanded.

"An emergency in town," Cestov said. "Maldost, did you see Macduk leave here?"

The Afbera looked around as if realizing for the first time that the banker was no longer present.

"No. I was watching the front door the entire time, and no one left."

"Why didn't you stop him from entering the house?" Cestov demanded, and she put a shaky hand on his tail.

"It's not his fault—it's mine. I let him in. It's all my fault, and now Charlie..." Her words trailed off as tears choked her throat.

Cestov's tail circled her shoulders reassuringly.

"If it's anyone's fault, it's my fault," he said. "I should never have left you."

Plovac came in a moment later. "He's not sure, but one of the Granicans thought he saw someone leaving through the back door of the barn."

"Why the hell didn't he stop him?"

"He thought it was just one of the ranch hands. He had a sack of grain over his shoulder."

"Charlie!" Mariah cried.

"Fuck. Of course." He turned back to Plovac. "Did he see which way he went?"

"He thinks he was headed for the back pasture."

"The back pasture?" Maldost asked. "There's nothing back there but the yearling calves."

"And the ship," Cestov said, his voice quiet.

A whole new layer of terror opened up. What if he managed to get Charlie off the planet? How would they ever find one small boy in a whole galaxy of possibilities?

"Cestov," she whispered.

"Do not be afraid, my miri. I'm getting him back." He turned to the other men. "You stay here. If anyone other than me tries to come through that door, shoot them."

With a hard kiss to Mariah's lips and a gentle caress of Claire's head, he was gone.

## CHAPTER TWENTY-SIX

Devorat met him as he emerged from the house.
"No sign of trouble and Macduk's wagon is still parked out front." He shook his head. "I'm so sorry. Even though you said it was one of us, I didn't really believe it. And Macduk has always been such an upstanding member of our community."

"I did not suspect him either, but there's no time to blame ourselves now. Have the men surround the house. No one goes in. No one, Devorat, not even your most trusted man."

The male nodded grimly. "And what of you?"

"I'm going after my son."

"You need an escort."

He hesitated, his trust still shaken, but as he looked at his foreman's worried face, he relented.

"Only you and your brothers," he insisted. "And stay out of sight. I do not want to scare him and risk having him hurt Charlie."

"You got it. We'll flank your position." Devorat hurried away and Cestov set off for the back pasture at a run.

The *Wanderer* laid across the field like a giant exotic insect, the pockmarked metal skin an odd contrast to the soft purple vegetation. As soon as he got close enough, he saw Macduk sitting by the closed door to the landing ramp, by all appearances resting comfortably in the shade of the ship.

"Where's my son?" he growled.

"Right here—so I suggest you don't come any closer." Macduk gestured to the grain sack lying at his feet and the rage that swept over him turned the world red.

"Get him out of there," he said through gritted teeth.

"Are you sure? He's much easier to control like this. He kept wanting to put up a fuss even though I told him everything would be fine as long as he obeyed me."

"Get him out of there. Now."

"Oh, very well." For a moment, the male's smiling demeanor disappeared. "But if you come any closer, I'll wring his little neck. Do you understand?"

Cestov forced himself to nod and Macduk smiled again, once more the friendly banker. He opened the sack and Cestov's heart twisted at the sight of Charlie lying in a small heap at the bottom. A tear-stained face looked up as the fabric fell away and Charlie's eyes met his.

"Daddy!" he cried and started to leap up, but Macduk caught his shoulder.

"Now, you just be still, boy. Your daddy and I have some business to discuss."

Cestov could see the male's meaty hand digging into his son's fragile shoulder and he resolved to break every one of those fat fingers.

"It's all right, Charlie," he said as calmly as possible. "I'm here now."

"Daddy," Charlie whispered again, more tears rolling down his small cheeks.

"What do you want, Macduk?"

"I want off this godsdamned planet. I'm so fucking tired of all these nice, friendly people. You may have burnt this crop, but I sold the previous two and I have quite enough money to let me explore some more... interesting ways of life."

"You had my brother killed, didn't you?"

Macduk waved his hand. "He shouldn't have poked his nose in where it didn't belong. I was even going to let him keep this ranch as long as he kept the cattle out of the hills, but he wouldn't listen to me and he was getting the townspeople all stirred up."

Anger and sorrow fought for dominance at hearing his suspicions were confirmed.

"I'm going to kill you," he promised.

The male looked unfazed by the threat. "No, you're not. You're going to get me off this planet."

"What makes you think I'd ever help you?"

"Because I have the boy and I think you'll do whatever I say rather than see him harmed. We are going to get on board this ship and you're going to take me to the nearest system with a large interstellar port. Provided you're an obedient pilot, I'll let you and the boy go as soon as we arrive. I won't even try and sell him to make up for what you've cost me. Although I could probably get a good price for him," he added thoughtfully.

"You're not going to sell my son."

"I'd be willing to give you a share. I know you Cires are desperate to carry on your race, but let's face it. He's not really your son, is he?"

"Am too!" Charlie scowled and, in a sudden burst of toddler fury, kicked wildly at Macduk. It couldn't possibly have hurt him, but it distracted the banker as he tried to yank Charlie away from his leg. He snatched him up, shaking him, and Charlie promptly vomited all over him. Macduk gave a horrified cry and dropped him, but Cestov was there. He caught Charlie and tucked him behind his back, his tail keeping the boy safe as his own hands went to Macduk's neck.

"This is for my brother," he growled, and in one quick move broke the man's neck.

Part of him regretted the swiftness of the death— the male deserved to suffer—but the little boy at his back was more important. He dropped to his knees, pulling Charlie into his arms and shielding him from the sight of the body.

"D-Daddy," Charlie sobbed into his neck—wet, dirty, and infinitely precious.

"It's all right, son. Everything is over now."

"You are my daddy! You are."

"Yes, Charlie, I am. For always."

A sound made him look up, his hand going to his gun, but it was only Devorat and his brothers approaching. Devorat shook his head as he stared down at the body.

"Never would have expected that."

"He played his part very well," Cestov agreed as his anger finally dissipated, leaving behind only sorrow. "I'm going to take the little one back to the house. I know my mate will be worrying herself sick."

"Mama," Charlie whispered. "The bad man hurt Mama."

"She's fine, Charlie," he said with a reassuring hug. "She fell asleep for a little while and now she's waiting for you."

"Wanna see Mama."

"We're going right now." He looked at Devorat. "Can you take care of him?"

"Yeah." Devorat gestured to two of his brothers, then turned to accompany Cestov back towards the house. "Do you think the marshal was in on it?"

"I suspect he got paid to whitewash my brother's death. Other than that, I do not know."

"Time for a town meeting," the foreman said, his tone grim. "I'll spread the word."

"My guess is they already know it's needed." He told an outraged Devorat about the incident with Radna.

Charlie was half asleep in his arms, worn out from terror, by the time he reached the house, but he revived when he saw Mariah. She came flying out of the house as soon as they approached.

"Mama," he cried and threw himself into her arms with a fresh wave of tears. Mariah was crying just as hard and he enclosed the two of them in his arms. Thank Granthar, he had his family back safely.

When they finally calmed down, Mariah drew back and smiled at Charlie.

"I think you need a bath, little one."

"Don't wanna."

"The sooner you have one, the sooner we can have milk and cookies by the fire."

He considered it, tilting his head speculatively. "You gonna sing?"

"Yes, Charlie. I'll sing for you."

Cestov followed them into the house, only to find Maldost with Devoji sitting on his lap. The girl blushed and started to get up, but Maldost kept his arm around her.

"We are to be mated," Maldost said with an odd combination of pride and belligerence.

He hid his smile. "I am very happy for you both."

Claire started kicking her feet at the sound of his voice and he went to pick her up, cradling her gently against his chest. She cooed happily, but he felt a sudden need to have his entire family together after the terror of the afternoon.

"I'm going to check on Mariah and Charlie. Carry on with, uh, whatever you were doing."

Maldost grinned and Devoji blushed.

In their bedroom, he sat Claire up amongst the pillows, her big blue eyes searching the room. He could hear Mariah and Charlie in the next room, his son seeming to have already recovered more than he expected. Thank Granthar that nothing more serious had happened to him. An indignant squeal came from the hallway and he looked up to see Lilat trotting towards him. He laughed and scooped her up on the bed as well.

"Are you feeling neglected, little one? It has been a chaotic day."

The slonga examined his face and neck with her trunk, then turned around twice, before settling down in front of Claire. His daughter cooed and grabbed a handful of pink fur. Lilat grunted but remained at the baby's feet, her trunk patting gently at Claire's hands.

When Mariah emerged from the bathing room with a clean Charlie wrapped in towels, he laughed. She looked as if she had been the one to take the bath, fully clothed. Although, he did appreciate the way the wet cloth clung to her skin and the way her nipples peaked beneath her damp shirt.

"That is an interesting look, my miri."

"Your son likes to splash."

"Splash!" Charlie yelled.

"Maybe you should give him a bath next time," she added dryly.

"I would be honored."

She rolled her eyes, depositing Charlie on the bed before she turned to the closet to pull out a dry outfit.

"Sing, Mama," Charlie said when she returned.

"All right," she agreed and joined them on the bed. Softly, she sang a song he remembered from before. A song about it being a wonderful world. As he looked around at his family, safe in his arms once more, he couldn't agree more.

## CHAPTER TWENTY-SEVEN

"Damn," Mariah said as she pulled yet another failed pie from the oven.

"Damn," Charlie echoed from where he was sitting at the table coloring.

"Don't say that, sweetheart. It's a grown-up word."

"I'm a big boy."

"You are, but not that big yet."

"When?"

"When you're as tall as Daddy." She dropped a kiss on his head as she went to dispose of the pie. She offered Lilat a piece but even the slonga turned up her trunk. Her efforts did not seem to be getting any better. Thank goodness Devoji and Maldost had decided to stay on at the ranch.

*I guess this is home now*, she thought and tried to suppress a feeling of gloom. It wasn't so much the planet—in the month since Macduk's death, she had become better acquainted with many in the local community. They had rallied together to send Marshal Zakon packing and with Macduk dead, the Dhalecs had left as well.

A surprising number of people had come out to the ranch to give her their condolences and express their shock over the banker's behavior. She had enjoyed the visits and felt somewhat isolated once they ceased. If only they were a little closer to town... She shook her head. If wishes were horses, beggars would ride. How many times had she heard Judith say that? She rubbed the friendship bracelet nestled next to hers. She still thought of her sister often but now her memories warmed rather than hurt.

"No pie?" Charlie asked, bringing her back to the present.

"No, I'm afraid not. Let's see how dinner looks."

She had the kitchen to herself today. Devoji and Maldost had gone for a ride. Supposedly to see if they could find a good location to build a small house, but she suspected they would use the time alone for a lot more than that. Her own time alone with Cestov seemed to be in short supply. He felt obligated to oversee the work on the ranch and spent a vast amount of time outside—time she was sure he didn't enjoy, although he never complained. Neither one of them seemed really cut out for ranch life she thought, as she lifted a lid and saw the unappetizing results of the stew she'd tried to make.

"It sure would be nice to be able to call out for pizza for a change," she muttered.

A moment later, Devoji and Maldost came into the kitchen laughing.

"How are things going?" Devoji asked.

"About as well as can be expected."

The girl pulled off the lid and couldn't hide her expression quickly enough. "Why don't you let me take over?"

"You're supposed to have the day off," she protested.

"It's fine. Maldost wants to go check on one of the robedas who is ailing anyway."

The Afbera grinned and gave his mate a quick kiss. "I'll be back in time for dinner."

"I'll have it waiting," she promised.

Mariah stared after him. He seemed so at home here, as if he had been born on this planet.

"Don't you mind?" she asked Devoji.

"Mind what?"

"That he's always disappearing off on ranch business?"

"Why should I? I have my own work to do."

Devoji began sautéing vegetables in a clean pot. Mariah could have sworn she had done the same thing, but it already smelled better than her attempt.

"Any luck on finding a good location for the house?"

The girl shrugged. "Not yet. We don't want to be too far away, but we need a water supply and a reasonably flat plot. And then, of course, we have to build. I don't believe we'll be able to have the mating ceremony until the spring."

"You know you're welcome to stay here."

"I know and I thank you. But Maldost wants us to have our own place." She blushed.

"I can understand that," she said sympathetically. That was another of the downsides of the ranch—between the constant business of running the ranch and the numbers of hands they employed, it seemed like people were always coming in and out.

*Stop it*, she told herself. This is Judith and Bratan's legacy.

Cestov appeared in the kitchen doorway and her heart did its usual somersault. He was one part of this new life that she never regretted.

"Daddy," Charlie squealed and launched himself across the room. Cestov caught him easily and she smiled as the big green head and small blond one touched foreheads. Claire squeaked from her cradle, her little fists waving. Cestov picked her up as well, then walked across the kitchen to kiss Mariah.

"Hello, my miri."

"You're back early."

"One of the hands was telling me that all four moons will be aligned tonight, and I thought it would be nice to share that with the children. And with you, of course."

His tail curved around her waist and pulled her closer. "Perhaps we can have a private viewing after they are asleep," he whispered.

A shiver went down her spine, her nipples already tightening in anticipation.

"That sounds wonderful. When does it start?"

"Just before dusk. Can we have an early meal?"

"Since Devoji has taken over, I'm sure that won't be a problem," she said dryly. "Is that all right with you, Devoji?"

"Of course. I'll have it on the table in a few minutes," the girl said cheerfully.

Mariah smiled gratefully but couldn't help feeling a pang of envy. If only Devoji weren't quite so efficient and if only she weren't failing quite so badly at being a rancher's mate.

"Is everything all right, Mariah?" Cestov asked quietly.

She forced another smile. "Just fine. Let's get everyone ready."

As they gathered in the back pasture as night fell, Cestov couldn't help casting a wistful glance at the place where his ship had resided. Plovac and Servisa had taken her to the big port on the lower part of the continent to see about trading the rest of the cargo. Once the hold was empty, he would have to think about selling her. He hated the idea, but he was a rancher now and a rancher did not need a ship.

"You sad, Daddy?" Charlie asked.

"Perhaps a little. I was thinking about the *Wanderer*."

"Gone to the stars?"

"No, just to Port Luka."

"Wanna go to the stars," Charlie said firmly.

"And one day you can. But you like the ranch, right?"

Charlie shrugged, his gaze still fixed on the heavens. How ironic that his brother's son seemed to long to travel as much as Cestov had once done. He's just a little boy, he reminded himself. He'll probably change his mind. Still, as the moons started to align, he took Charlie's hand and walked up a slight hill, so they could see the whole sky, the endless galaxy waiting for them. The two large moons hung high overhead, while the two smaller ones chased along their edge. Charlie watched, wide-eyed with wonder.

"Do you know that in ancient times, sailors used the moon and the stars to find their way?" he asked, still thinking about his ship.

"Sailors? Like Mama's song?"

"Yes, just like that."

He thought of the sextant—their family legacy—in Bratan's office. "I'll show you how. Would you like that?"

"Yeah," Charlie said and the two of them watched in silence as the heavens danced.

When the show was over, he carried a sleepy Charlie to bed. He changed Claire's diaper and handed her to Mariah for her last feeding while he went to find the sextant. He pulled the case off the shelf and lifted the instrument out. As he did, he heard the rustle of paper. He lifted the lining and saw a sheet of old-fashioned paper covered with his brother's familiar handwriting. A reminiscent smile twisted his lips. Bratan had always loved the feel of paper and ink. He unfolded the sheet and his heart skipped a beat. It was a letter addressed to him.

. . .

Dear Cestov,

You must forgive me for having waited such a horribly long time before contacting you. At first, I was too hurt and angry, but as time passed, I realized that I was just as much to blame. I should have stayed, should have explained to you how much the idea of a mate and family meant to me. But even then, in my stubborn pride, I was determined to wait until I could show you that it was possible.

I will admit that I had begun to give up hope, but then I stumbled on to an underground market and one of those despicable Vedeckians. He was trying to sell a female and a child. As you can imagine, I was horrified, and I interceded with no thought except to prevent such a tragedy. But then... Cestov, Father was completely and utterly wrong. She is my mate and I have taken her son as my own. She is not Cire, but she is beautiful and sweet and funny and loving and—well, you understand.

Although she loves me as well, she mourns for the planet she left behind and even more for a sister that she loves, but I do not know where to find that planet. I am ashamed to admit that it did not occur to me to question the Vedeckian until it was too late. I cannot erase that mistake but I am determined to provide a home for her and so we have settled on Granica. It is a peaceful planet and I hope that you will come and visit us.

Father was wrong about something else as well. My mate and I have been blessed with a child. A beautiful, perfect daughter who reflects our love. She needs to meet her uncle and you need to know that these things are possible. Perhaps you do not want them, but I suspect that despite your harsh words, you would be overjoyed to find these same blessings.

*I will send this the next time an interstellar trader comes to our small town and hope that it finds you quickly. I am sending it with the sextant in hopes that it will help guide your path. And I hope that your path will lead you to visit us. Perhaps you will not stay, perhaps you will not approve of the life I have chosen, but I hope that the bonds between us can be restored.*

*I am very sorry about what happened between us, my brother, but I think of you often.*

*With love,*
*Bratan*

MARIAH FOUND HIM THERE, STILL STARING AT THE letter.

"Is something wrong? I thought you were coming to bed."

"I found a letter. From my brother."

"Oh." She came over and perched on his lap, wrapping her arms around his neck. "Is it a good letter?"

"A very good one." He handed it to her. "Can you read this?"

"I think so. The reader you gave me has taught me a lot."

When she finished, her eyes were wet with tears. "I'm so glad he was trying to get in touch with you."

"I wish I had found him earlier."

"I know." She put a gentle hand on his cheek. "I wish I could have seen Judith again."

"There was something else in the case. Here." He handed her the small image. Judith was lying in the bed, a radiant smile on her face as she looked down at Claire. Bratan sat beside her, one arm around her and the other around Charlie who was leaning eagerly towards the new baby. His brother looked so proud and so content.

"They look so happy." She stroked her finger down her sister's face. "As happy as we are."

"Yes," he agreed, but his brother's words echoed in his mind. Was his true legacy not the ranch, but the ability to follow his own stars?

# CHAPTER TWENTY-EIGHT

A week later, Mariah flicked through her limited wardrobe, trying to decide on the appropriate outfit for a visit to town. Cestov had been several times this week and had been extremely mysterious about his purpose. She suspected that he was getting ready to sell the *Wanderer* but didn't want to discuss it. She knew how much it bothered him to let it go, but they really didn't need a ship when they had a ranch. She tried not to think of it as leaving them trapped on Granica. After all, she had spent her whole life on Earth and never felt the need to leave.

When she finally emerged, Cestov was waiting impatiently. He had an air of suppressed excitement that tickled her curiosity, but she had already decided that she wouldn't press him. He obviously intended to surprise her with something.

After pacifying a pouting Charlie with the promise of a treat from town, they set out in the wagon.

"It really is a pretty planet, isn't it?" she asked as they wound through the gently rolling purple hills. "I guess there are worse places we could have ended up."

"Much worse," he agreed, then shot her a worried look. "Do you miss Earth?"

"I miss some things. Some of the places I sang. Takeout pizza. The beach. I suppose all of the things I was familiar with—but you are more important to me than any of them."

"I'm glad." His tail circled her wrist and she put her hand over it.

They spent the rest of the trip talking idly about nothing of great importance. The trip somehow reminded her of setting off for one of her music tours and she found herself singing to him. He had picked up the words to some of the songs and she loved to hear him harmonize, his deep voice complimenting hers.

When they arrived in town, to her surprise, he didn't turn down the main street, but followed one of the back roads. He pulled up outside a gated wall.

"What's this?"

"A surprise."

She gave him a suspicious look but let him help her down from the wagon. With his tail firmly around her waist, he led her through the gate and into a garden surrounded by high walls that stretched from the gate to a two-story building.

"Oh, this is beautiful." One side of the garden had a swath of low purple grass, while the other held flowering bushes arranged around patio with a small fountain and… "Look, they have a sundial just like ours."

A smile flashed across his face. "Yes, they do."

He led her up onto the veranda that spanned the length of the building and through a set of glass doors. A big open living space greeted her with a fireplace at one end and a kitchen at the other, equipped with the same cooking machines she had seen on Cestov's ship. She gave them an envious stare.

"I don't understand. Whose house is this and why are we here?"

"I'll explain in a minute."

He led her up a set of wide stairs to show her three small sunny bedrooms and a big bedroom overlooking the rear garden. Another set of stairs and they emerged on the flat roof of the building. A waist-high balustrade circled the space, but she could see out over most of the town to the land beyond, rolling gently towards the mountains. Part of the roof was shaded by a pergola and a set of comfortable looking furniture promised an inviting spot to sit and admire the view.

"Okay, Cestov. Talk to me," she said, leading him to the couch.

"Do you like the house?" he asked as they sat down.

"Of course I do. I could see us living here—if we didn't live at the ranch, I mean."

"Is that what you want? To live at the ranch?"

He was studying her so closely that even though her first impulse was to assure him that she did, she found herself giving him a rueful smile. "Not really. I know that's terrible and it's the children's legacy and I'm fine with staying there. It's just not really..."

"A perfect fit?"

"Exactly. Devoji is so good at everything and I'm just not."

"Your skills lie in other areas."

"Not areas that are appreciated at the ranch." That wasn't entirely true. She still frequently sang in the evenings, but it wasn't quite the same as singing for an audience.

"I have been thinking that perhaps we should move to town," he said slowly.

Her heart skipped a beat. She loved the idea of being around more people, of finding her own place again, but...

"But what about the ranch?"

"If you are willing, I thought I would give Maldost the opportunity to go into partnership with us. I can loan him the money to get started and he can pay me back from his share of the profits. He and Devoji would continue to live there while we moved into town."

"What about the children?"

"I'm not sure that Charlie is really that interested in ranch life," he said slowly. "I know he's young and that could easily change. If it does, we can decide on a course of action at that time. With Claire also, if she expresses an interest."

Excitement swept over her, but she forced herself to slow down and think about the consequences. "What about you? What will you do? You're not going to take the Marshal's job, are you?"

The town had offered him the job after Marshal Zakon was sent away and she had been relieved when he refused, afraid that his sense of responsibility would have compelled him to take the position.

"I offered to go into partnership with Radna." He smiled at her. "I am a trader at heart, after all."

"And he agreed?"

"Yes. Subject to your approval, of course. Since the incident with Macduk, he would prefer to be able to take life a little more easily. He even offered to convert one of the backrooms into a place where you could perform if you wished."

*If she wished?* She could think of nothing that would make her happier. She had only one other concern.

"But what about your ship?"

He grinned, his happiness obvious. "A merchant always needs a source of supplies. Plovac and Servisa can handle the trading runs or we can hire some additional crew if they need them. We could even go with them sometimes when the children are older."

An answering excitement rose in her own heart, but she

put her hand on his cheek and studied his face. "You're really sure about this?"

"Yes, my miri. My brother was sending me the sextant to guide my path - my path, not his. And this feels right to me. But only if it makes you happy as well?"

Make her happy? To live in this bright little house, close to everything? To be able to sing? To have the promise of more trips amongst the stars?

"Nothing could make me happier."

"Good."

He lifted her into his arms, kissing her until she was breathless and rubbing her nipples against his hard chest, seeking to relieve the throbbing ache. His tail crept up to pull the needy peaks as he lowered her back on the couch.

"Oh, I left out one important detail." He smiled down at her.

"Yes," she said absently, reaching for the fastening of his pants.

"The store is right across the street. That means I'll always be close by."

"I want you closer now," she whispered as she freed his erection, the heavy length springing into her hand. She gave it a long slow stroke and he groaned.

"I will not last if you keep doing that," he warned.

"You can't handle a little teasing?" she asked innocently.

"Can you?"

He flipped her onto her back and proceeded to kiss and stroke every part of her until her whole body was on fire with longing, until he finally, finally drove into her and her vision sheeted white as she convulsed in helpless ecstasy, until he knotted deep inside, his seed filling her.

. . .

Afterwards, they lay locked together in contented satisfaction. She looked up through the pergola slats at the deep lavender-blue sky. Not an Earth sky but that no longer mattered. She had found her home, she had found her family, and wherever she traveled from now on, she would never be alone.

# EPILOGUE

O*ne year later...*

"Mariah, are you ready?" Cestov strode into the dressing room, looking every bit as handsome as he had the first day they met. Her heart skipped a beat as her body responded the way it always did to the sight of her warrior.

"Yes, I'm ready." She lifted her hand towards him, her new collection of bracelets jingling with the movement. Once he had realized how much she enjoyed the jewelry, he and the children had provided her with a new bracelet on every occasion. But the most significant one was still the first one. When he found her crying over her sister's bracelet after another one of the threads snapped, he had carefully painted the fraying threads with a clear liquid which would preserve them forever. She pressed a finger against it now. *Love you, Ju*, she thought.

He took her outstretched hand and helped her carefully to her feet. The increasingly large bulge of her stomach tended to throw her off balance and she appreciated his assistance. When they had decided to try for a child, both of them had been afraid to get their hopes up but she was pregnant within a week. Whovian had taken over the medical center in Selo and he had confirmed her pregnancy with a small but genuine smile. He seemed to have finally laid his demons to rest.

"You look more beautiful than ever, my mate," Cestov said, admiring her.

She gave a careful twirl, loving the way her new skirts swished out. Most of the women on Granica tended to prefer more practical pants, but she had missed the easy flow of her old outfits. In the end, with a lot of swearing and considerable assistance from Devoji, she had managed to make herself a few skirts for performance nights.

"Are there a lot of people out there?" she asked nervously.

"Of course, there are. You know that everyone wants to hear you sing. You are a star."

To her surprise, it was true. Maybe it was the overall lack of entertainment or maybe it was because she was part of this community now, but the room was always packed to the edges when she sang. A few of the townspeople had even been discussing putting up a larger hall now that people sometimes came from the outlying settlements and even other towns for her monthly performances. How ironic to find the kind of musical success she had always wanted in a small town on an alien planet. Success and motherhood—which reminded her of their son.

"What's Charlie doing? You know he can get into trouble the minute we're not watching him."

Cestov laughed. "Do not worry. Maldost is following him around while Devoji looks after Claire and her own baby, and Lilat keeps an eye on all of them."

They had tried leaving the slonga at the ranch, afraid she

would be unhappy in town, but after the third time she had escaped and tried to follow them, they had given in and brought her with them. She seemed perfectly content in the townhouse, even though the number of slonga at the ranch had increased. After some fairly extensive negotiations with the government of Srashiman, instead of returning Tajka and the others, Maldost had been given permission to start a herd of slonga on Granica. Three additional females and a very impressive male had joined them on the ranch.

"It's so great having Maldost and Devoji visit us. You don't suppose they would be willing to move into town permanently, do you?"

They both laughed. The young couple seemed more than content out on the ranch. Cestov was still the majority partner, but Maldost paid off a little bit more of the loan each month.

Radna appeared in the doorway. "Everyone's waiting."

The little shopkeeper had become more than just a business partner; he had become a friend and an honorary grandfather. She smiled at him.

"I'm ready."

Her mate took her hand and led her to where her audience waited.

"Mama!" Claire squealed as Mariah walked up on the small stage. The people sitting near them gave her an amused glance, but Charlie gently placed a finger on her lips.

"Hush, Claire. Mama's gonna sing."

She gave him her big-eyed stare then nodded solemnly. Both children settled back against him as he wrapped his tail around them. Lilat reached up with her trunk, patting each small figure to make sure that they were safe. *Not so small anymore,* he thought. How fast they had grown. Claire was taking her first tottering steps and Charlie seemed to have doubled in size. His gaze went from the children to his mate, her head bent over the strings of the dobron as she started to sing, the swell of her stomach a reminder that their family was expanding. Not a future he had ever dreamed of, but one that filled him with joy every day.

Bratan had tried to tell him and he had been too stubborn to listen. *You were right, my brother,* he thought. *And I will make sure that your family—*our *family—can follow their own dreams.*

LATER THAT EVENING, CESTOV JOINED MARIAH ON THE roof of their building. She was dancing slowly, her bare feet moving to the rhythm of her humming and he remembered the first time he brought her to his cabin. She had been beautiful and entrancing then, but she was so much more so now that he knew her as a companion, a mother, a mate. He waited until she grew closer, then twirled her into his arms, his tail wrapping around her waist as she lifted her arms to his neck.

"Happy, my miri?" he asked.

"More than I ever thought I'd be."

He pulled her closer, delighting in the soft warmth of her body, of the new life blossoming between them. Mariah's steps slowed and she led him over to the edge of the roof, looking not up at the stars, but at the small town laid out before them.

"I spent my whole life fighting to avoid this destiny," she said softly.

"As did I."

"How Judith would laugh."

Her eyes sparkled in the moonlight and he saw a tear glisten on her cheek.

"Bratan would have laughed as well, but I know they would

both be glad to know that we are here together and that their children are loved and happy."

"To our family," she said, raising an imaginary glass.

He took her back into his arms, wrapping them around the swollen mound of her stomach.

"To our family," he echoed. "To the ones who are here, to the ones who are yet to come, and to the ones who live on in our hearts."

Her hands tightened over his and together they looked out over their home as they swayed to the music that only the two of them could hear.

# AUTHORS' NOTE

Thank you for reading **A Son for the Alien Warrior**! We hope you enjoyed seeing another Cire Warrior and his human mate discover that no matter where you are in the universe, love is all you need to create a family.

As always, there are so many people to thank!

To our fantastic readers... Your unbelievable support and love of **Mama and the Alien Warrior** inspired us to continue the *Treasured by the Alien* series. Thank you! While there is no set date for our next release, there is definitely more to come! You may have noticed that there is another human female with a story to be discovered...

To our awesome beta readers: Kathryn S., Tammy S., Janet S., Annie T., and Kitty S.... You ladies rock! Thank you!

To our fabulous cover designers: Cameron Kamenicky and Naomi Lucas... Oh, sweet alien tail! You guys did it again! So well done! Thank you!

To our loving families... We couldn't do it without you! Thank you from the bottom of our hearts.

Thank you again for reading our book! Whether you

## AUTHORS' NOTE

enjoyed the story or not, it would mean the world to us if you left an honest review at Amazon. Reviews help other readers find books to enjoy, which helps the authors as well!

All the best,
Honey & Bex

---

If you would like to be kept up to date on all the latest news—including release dates—please sign up for our newsletters!

Sign up for Honey's newsletter at www.honeyphillips.com!
Sign up for Bex's newsletter at www.bexmclynn.com!

## OTHER TITLES

**Treasured by the Alien**

by Honey Phillips and Bex Mclynn

*Mama and the Alien Warrior*

*A Son for the Alien Warrior*

**Cosmic Fairy Tales**

*The Ugly Dukeling* by Bex McLynn

*Jackie and the Giant* by Honey Phillips

**Books by Honey Phillips**

**The Alien Abduction Series**

*Anna and the Alien*

*Beth and the Barbarian*

*Cam and the Conqueror*

*Deb and the Demon*

*Ella and the Emperor*

*Faith and the Fighter*

*Greta and the Gargoyle*

**The Alien Invasion Series**

*Alien Selection*

*Alien Conquest*

*Alien Prisoner*

*Alien Breeder*

*Alien Alliance*

*Alien Hope*

## Cyborgs on Mars

*High Plains Cyborg*

*The Good, the Bad, and the Cyborg*

## Books by Bex McLynn

## The Ladyships Series

*Sarda*

*Thanemonger*

*Bane*

## Standalone

*Rein: A Tidefall Novel*

Made in the USA
Middletown, DE
15 July 2020